Wade Stone's gray hid part of his face, but **she didn't need to see his eyes to know he had changed.**

When Amy had known him, he was gangly and not yet a man. There was nothing boyish about him as he stood before her now. His broad shoulders were squared. He looked powerful and a little wary. His wool jacket was open, a flashy silver belt buckle with a rodeo scene all too visible.

"I'm sorry," Wade said, his voice low and tense. She turned to look at him. Was he going to apologize? For leaving her? After all this time? Then he continued. "My mother shouldn't have offered you the job. It's a lot of work—hard work—and it's just not for you."

A shadow of whiskers covered his face, showing he hadn't shaved this morning. His jaw was tense.

Amy lifted her chin. "I'm stronger than you think."

He looked at her for a long moment. "You'll regret it."

"I don't think so," she said, looking him square in the eyes.

Books by Janet Tronstad

Love Inspired

*An Angel for Dry Creek
*A Gentleman for Dry Creek
*A Bride for Dry Creek
*A Rich Man for Dry Creek
*A Hero for Dry Creek
*A Baby for Dry Creek
*A Dry Creek Christmas
*Sugar Plums for Dry Creek
*At Home in Dry Creek
†The Sisterhood of the
  Dropped Stitches
*A Match Made in Dry Creek
*Shepherds Abiding in Dry Creek
†A Dropped Stitches Christmas
*Dry Creek Sweethearts
†A Heart for the Dropped Stitches
*A Dry Creek Courtship
*Snowbound in Dry Creek
†A Dropped Stitches Wedding
*Small-Town Brides
  "A Dry Creek Wedding"
*Silent Night in Dry Creek
*Wife Wanted in Dry Creek
Doctor Right
*Small-Town Moms
  "A Dry Creek Family"
*Sleigh Bells for Dry Creek

Love Inspired Historica

*Calico Christmas at Dry Creek
*Mistletoe Courtship
  "Christmas Bells for Dry Creek"

*Dry Creek
†Dropped Stitches

JANET TRONSTAD

grew up on a farm in central Montana, spending many winter days reading books. None of those books were as eagerly consumed as the ones about Christmas. Stars. Sleighs. The story of the Christ Child being born. She loved them all. That's why, almost every year since she started writing the Dry Creek series, there's a new Christmas book. Janet lives in Pasadena, California, where she is a full-time writer.

Sleigh Bells for Dry Creek
Janet Tronstad

Love Inspired

Recycling programs
for this product may
not exist in your area.

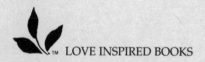

LOVE INSPIRED BOOKS

ISBN-13: 978-0-373-08209-4

SLEIGH BELLS FOR DRY CREEK

www.LoveInspiredBooks.com

Printed in U.S.A.

And ye shall know the truth,
and the truth shall make you free.
—*John* 8:32

This book is dedicated to my friends
in the Fort Shaw Bible church, located in
central Montana. They are making the
long journey together, the bumps in the road
and all. I wish them a Merry Christmas.

Chapter One

Wade Stone stopped his pickup at the edge of Dry Creek, Montana, and peered through the icy windshield. The December sky was dark, as much from the storm clouds as from the slowness of the dawn. He turned his headlights off and could still clearly see the small town. A few weathered buildings with chipped paint and sagging porches lined each side of what passed for a street. Most people would travel through Dry Creek and forget all about it by the time they reached the state line.

But not Wade.

Even though he had been gone for nine years, one look at this town reminded him of how much he missed it. He was weary of living out of motels and following the rodeo circuit. At twenty-six years old, he had yet to find a place that measured up to Dry Creek, and he was ready to settle down.

He glanced over at his mother, sitting so still in the passenger side of the seat. It didn't matter how he felt; he and his family were not welcome here. They couldn't expect to come back and pretend the past was wiped clean just because his mother had served her jail time. In a place like this, people took murder seriously. They wouldn't soon forget that she'd killed her husband.

By now, his mother must realize her desire to come back wasn't going to work. He should have said something earlier, but her request that he drive her to the café had caught him off guard. He'd only returned to the family ranch last night, and he hadn't thought through some of these things. But now that he had, he'd just turn his pickup around and leave before anyone knew they had even been here.

He was all set to do that when, out of the grayness of the dawn, a sudden flurry of hail came quick and hard. The tiny hail-stones hit his windshield in a fast rhythm and, just when he became worried they'd actually do some damage, the storm stopped. Everything seemed strangely peaceful for a moment, and then a shaft of light came streaming right through the dark clouds.

Wade heard an indrawn breath and looked over at his mother again.

"That's God's message to me—that light in the darkness," she said, turning to him with relief shining on her face. "I was right to come back. It's a sign from Him."

Wade held his tongue. He didn't begrudge his mother the faith she'd found in prison. After all, he knew people did what they had to do to survive in those kinds of places. He'd done some foolish things himself after her trial ended and he left the family ranch. He was seventeen and thought himself a man, but he bought his first packet of spearmint chewing gum just because the smell reminded him of that kiss he'd stolen from Amy Mitchell down the street from here. Sweet, golden-haired Amy. He'd never forget her.

Just having the gum had given him comfort in those early days when he had been sleeping in his pickup and trying to find his place in the rodeo world. The smell made him dream of a better life, even if he knew he'd never live it. He supposed it was like that for his mother and her newfound faith.

"It's winter. There's nothing unusual about this kind of day," Wade finally pointed out, trying to keep his voice soft. He understood her hope. He still had a packet of that gum in his shirt pocket.

The glow dimmed on his mother's face. By now, covered by more gray clouds, the light was gone from the sky, too.

"You think I'm wrong? To come back here?" she asked.

"No, I just meant—" He scrambled to find words to explain his unease and then couldn't bring himself to speak them. He might not share her faith, but his mother had suffered enough. "It doesn't need to mean anything. That's all."

Strands of white hair ran through his mother's formerly all-black mane, and her nose had the slight hook inherited from her Cherokee grandfather. Wade didn't need to look any closer to see she was fragile. She might be only forty-five years old, but unless she smiled, she could pass for sixty. He wondered if she'd gotten her full hour of exercise each day when she'd been away.

She searched his eyes for a moment. "Is that why your brothers aren't here?"

"Did you send them letters, too?"

She nodded and then looked out the window. Her face softened as though she was dreaming. "You might think I'm foolish to be here, but once our ranch is back in shape, there will be room for all of you boys to come home and make a life for yourself."

After nine years of standing empty, the ranch house was in shambles. Wade had looked around with a flashlight last night when he'd arrived. At least one of the windows had been broken, and an animal of some kind had gotten inside. Dishes sat in pieces on the kitchen floor and chewed-up paper had been blown into the corners of the living room. He hadn't been able to see the fields in the dark, but he imagined they weren't any better. He hadn't come back because he felt he could change anything on the old place. He only wanted to do what he could to spare his mother any more pain and humiliation. He owed her that much.

"Don't worry about my brothers and me. We have lives." He didn't see the need to go into details. He wasn't sure that his mother knew about Jake's recent string of gambling losses in Las Vegas. And none of them had heard from Tyler in a couple of years, so Wade assumed his youngest brother was having a hard time, too. There hadn't been a place in Montana, so both of his brothers had gone to live in some kind of state institution for juveniles in North Dakota when their mother went to prison. Wade had been old enough to be given a choice about going with them, and he had refused. His emotions had been so raw back then that he wanted to put everything behind him, including his family.

He hadn't been able to, though. He'd thought of his brothers more than he had wanted, even if he hadn't known what to say to either of them when he'd called. He wondered if his brothers blamed him for not sticking with them, but he'd never asked. He felt bad enough about it on his own.

"The barn is tight against the weather. We can all stay there if needed until the house is ready," his mother continued, as if it was a plan she'd worked out in her mind some time ago—and he guessed she probably had. She had been sleeping in the tack room off the barn for the few days she'd been back, and he figured that was mostly because the roof was good and there was an electrical outlet. She could plug in a lamp to read that Bible she carried everywhere with her.

Wade had unrolled his sleeping bag in one of the old stalls last night. He didn't need a light to read anything—religious or not—but he had lain there until midnight, watching the moonlight shine through the frost on the side window and wishing he could wipe away the past with a big, black book like his mother seemed to be doing.

He finally dozed off and managed to sleep for several hours before a spasm in his leg woke him. It was almost dawn and bitter cold, even inside the barn. When he stood, the cramp went away, but his leg was stiffer than usual. The rodeo doctor had said Wade would limp for a long time after his last fall, and it seemed that he was right.

"We'll talk about all of this later," Wade said now, keeping his voice gentle. His mother had her own wounds from the past, and he didn't want her to worry about any of his. "Let me take you home so you can rest."

"It won't get any easier." His mother pressed her lips into a severe line as her fingers gripped the edge of the metal bowl she held in her lap. "Besides, I've come to buy eggs. The café will surely sell me some."

He noticed with a start that she still had her gold wedding band on her finger.

"I told you I don't need breakfast." He

wondered if her knuckles were swollen, and that's why she hadn't taken the ring off. The round band had been cheap thirty years ago, and it had worn so thin since then that a wire cutter could slice through it like it was butter.

Just then, his mother's chin lifted, and he saw a glimpse of the woman she used to be. "It's your first morning back, and I intend to make you a sausage-and-egg scramble, like I did when you were a boy. We need to start living a normal life sometime."

He studied his mother for a long minute before suddenly realizing she probably hadn't even tried to remove that ring. She was stuck in the past. She didn't understand how things had changed.

"Come to Idaho with me," Wade urged suddenly. He'd competed in a rodeo there a couple of years ago, and he liked the state. It wasn't Dry Creek, but it had open spaces, and it would do fine. "I'll build us a nice, big house. One of those with a wraparound deck and maybe a sunroom just for you. Whatever you want. You like the sun."

She shook her head and smiled slightly. "Have I told you how proud I am of you? But you need to save your rodeo winnings for your own future. I have a home that suits me fine."

Wade knew better than to press her. No one in his family talked about their emotions with any ease, especially not with each other. "At least let me pay someone to help get the house in shape. I'll have my hands full with fixing the barn and corrals before I need to leave."

He'd started driving to Montana the day after he got her letter, but he didn't plan on staying so long that he missed the National Finals Rodeo next month. If he stopped riding for too long, he'd never get back on a horse again. That tumble he'd taken eight months ago had almost killed him. Since then, the other riders had decided he'd lost his nerve, and they had started circling his championship—the one he won every year—like buzzards in the dead of winter.

"I want to do the house myself," his mother said, dragging Wade's mind back to the conversation. "I need to get things ready for Christmas."

"Christmas?"

All thoughts of the championship fled Wade's mind. "Why would you—" He stopped when he saw his mother stiffen in protest. Then he tried again in a more reasonable voice. "I mean, that's less than a week away. Next Thursday, isn't it? There's no need to bother with a tree or lights or anything like that. It's too much work. And we never—"

"I know your father didn't celebrate Christmas," his mother interrupted with a quiet dignity. "But this year, I thought…" Her voice trailed off; she was probably lost in her own memories.

Wade shook his head. Saying his father didn't celebrate Christmas was like saying a rodeo bull didn't make a good household pet. The man had been vigilant about maintaining his ban on Christmas decorations. No holiday lights were allowed. Nothing red or green or gold was to be placed anywhere. No candles or pine cones were to be left on the fireplace mantel. Why, his father had once ripped the whole December page off the only calendar in the house, just because it had a small nativity scene on it.

"You always loved Christmas," his mother finally whispered.

Wade shrugged. His last words with his father had been angry ones spoken the day after Christmas nine years ago. "I make out fine without it."

Holidays were like the sweet visions that came to mind when he smelled spearmint gum. They were fine for other people but not for him. "Maybe I did like it back then, but you've got to remember that was a long time ago."

The argument with his father made Wade feel guilty every year when he heard the carols on the radio. Disagreements about Christmas had ruined what family he had. So now he never paused to admire a tree in a mall or a hotel. He sent no cards and got none in return. He wanted to forget all about December 25.

"You wanted to drive the sleigh. Remember?" his mother asked.

"I was just a boy."

He no more got the words out of his mouth than the memories came flooding back, whether he wanted them to or not. He could still see that red sleigh in his mind—the one that Charley Nelson used when he hauled hay to his range cattle during the big snowstorms that came up almost every winter in the eastern part of the state. Each Christmas, the man transformed that farm sleigh into a fairy tale worthy of the most fanciful child's dream. He painted holly sprigs on it one year and dancing elves another. And he always tacked the same string of sturdy iron bells along the sides, so people could hear it coming for miles around.

"You used to love that sleigh," his mother persisted.

Wade could only nod. He guessed he had, at that.

He had disobeyed his father every single year to go see it. Charley used a team of horses to pull the sleigh to the church around dusk on Christmas Eve. When he rang the bells, people came from all directions to fill it with presents for the annual children's gift drive. Then the sleigh sat there waiting while everyone walked over to the old barn at the edge of town to watch the nativity pageant. After that, Charley drove the sleigh around to deliver all the gifts.

Back then, the presents had been simple, handmade things, often wrapped in a brown grocery bag and tied with a single strip of red ribbon. No one had money for store-bought toys or fancy paper.

Wade and his brothers usually received a pair of warm mittens that Mrs. Hargrove, one of the church ladies, had knit. As hard as it was to believe now, those mittens had been enough to make Wade feel like he was a regular kid celebrating Christmas right along with all the other children in the world. On that one night, he wasn't one of the poor Stone boys; he was the same as everyone else. Someone had given him a Christmas gift.

All those years as a boy, Wade had willingly faced his father's wrath just to sneak into town and get the presents for him and his brothers. Charley always left the Stone family presents clearly marked on the seat of the sleigh so Wade could get them if he came early, before the pageant was finished.

Wade heard his mother sigh, and he looked over at her. He'd long since known he had been a fool to put so much stock in a day on the calendar.

"What happened to all of us?" she

asked, looking at him with discouragement on her face. "Just because I went to prison, that was no reason for you and your brothers to stop believing a good life is possible."

"We haven't stopped—"

"Not a one of you got married while I was gone," his mother interrupted him as though she knew what he was going to say and didn't want to even hear the rest of it. "I always thought you'd stay in touch with Amy, at least."

"She was just a kid back then," Wade protested and looked away, gripping the steering wheel as he did so. He might have liked Christmas, but his biggest weakness growing up had always been Amy. Even before he'd become aware of her as a girl, he'd known she was special in some way he couldn't define.

At first, she'd merely been underfoot, tagging along behind him, no matter whether he was helping his brothers move cattle or turning hay bales in the north pasture. His boyish pride made him complain about her being there, but his words were halfhearted. He wouldn't have admitted it, but he was always more content when she was around. She soothed something deep inside of him.

He felt bad about not saying a proper goodbye to her before he left, but none of his friends had known what his life had been like until the trial began. Before that, he had explained away his bruises and made light of his father's drunkenness. He had pretended his family was normal. But there was no hiding anything on the witness stand, and the Stone family problems were told and retold throughout the whole eastern part of the state. When the trial was over, it had been easier for him to climb into the family pickup and drive away, rather than face anyone with his shame.

His mother smiled. "I'm sure Amy's all grown up by now."

Before Wade could say anything more,

another pickup eased past and stopped directly in front of the café. He recognized the old, red Ford seconds before the driver's door opened and a woman stepped out. He wasn't more than ten feet behind her, but he still couldn't seem to make sense of the flash of shiny blond hair, twisted into some kind of a knot at the back of her head. A black work hat hung from her neck by a leather cord. Shapely, long legs filled out worn jeans. A heavy farm jacket swung free from her shoulders as she marched up to the café, determination in her every stride.

"It's Amy," his mother said, her voice blossoming with some kind of hope that made Wade want to slouch down in the seat so no one would be able to see him, even if the sun came out enough to clearly show him sitting inside his cab. Could it be? Was she still here?

He focused on the red-and-white bumper sticker on the back of the pickup. It urged everyone to vote for Garrett for the state legislature. Amy had just been learning to drive in that pickup when he'd left. He doubted she would have turned political. But then nine years had passed since he'd seen her. She could have turned into almost anything in that time.

"That's got to be Amy Mitchell," his mother repeated as she turned to look at him. "You can't tell me now that God doesn't want us in Dry Creek."

He didn't know how God felt about his presence here, but he was almost certain Amy wouldn't be too much in favor of it.

"You can't be sure that's her," he said, trying to hide the desperate lump in his throat.

Without warning, the picture of Amy's face came to him. He could still remember how her eyes had looked when he'd kissed her. She'd been fifteen and he'd been seventeen. Even now, just thinking about it, he could almost smell the spearmint gum she'd been chewing.

"We need to leave," he said to his mother.

His mouth was as dry as it had been that night. Reluctant to go anywhere after wrapping presents for the gift drive, he and Amy had been leaning against the closed back door of the church. It was one of the few times he'd been inside the church; no one in his family was a member, and he normally felt uneasy just being near the building. But on Christmas Eve, the church belonged to everyone. Or so he told himself, standing there on the porch.

Snow had started to fall. There was a light for the front door of the building, but none for the back one. Inside, people were practicing carols for the pageant. The moon was shining bright enough that he could see a single flake as it fell on Amy's nose. She giggled as he wiped it off. And then he kissed her. He hadn't planned it, but for a moment, he was glad he'd finally done it. He knew he'd never forget the feel of her lips on his and her soft hair falling across his hand.

Then he noticed her eyes had changed to a dark blue, almost like midnight. Her pupils were large and filled with some emotion he didn't recognize. Probably shock. She was not the kind of girl a guy kissed on the back steps of the church. He supposed it was against the rules of the place; Amy would know about that. She was always going to church, and she obeyed all the rules.

He wanted to reassure her, but when she kept staring up at him with her big, round eyes, he didn't know what to say. So, he said the first thing that came to mind. He said it was okay if they kissed on the steps, because he was going to marry her inside the church someday, anyway.

She was supposed to feel like that fact made the kiss more proper—surely the rules allowed for those kinds of kisses— but she turned so pale he thought she might faint. Obviously, the thought of marrying him didn't sit well with her, so he no longer had anything comforting to say. They just stood there for a moment, both stricken, until one of the guys in his class at school, Shawn Garrett, pushed open the back door and demanded to know what they were doing.

Shawn had never been a particular friend of his, but Wade was almost glad to see him that night. No one answered Shawn, but Amy slipped back inside the church and, the next time Wade saw her, her face had turned pink and she'd avoided his eyes. Of course, that had been after everything had happened, and he'd never been sure if it had been the murder or the kiss that had put her off him.

Wade kept looking at the bumper on the pickup. It must be Shawn's father who was running for the state legislature. Not that it mattered. Wade reached for the key hanging from the ignition. He was right the first time. If Amy was still around here, she had to be married to some rich rancher by now. Her Aunt Tilly always said Amy was destined for greatness, and Wade believed it. If he had any sense, he would start his pickup and drive until he and his mother were safely away from here. Amy could be married and doing great without them having to know about it.

"Well, I'm not going home without getting those eggs," his mother declared as she pressed down on the handle of her door. "Not when Amy might be inside."

"Wait," Wade breathed out in protest. He started to say more, but his mother was already out of the pickup and on her way to the café. A blast of cold air came in through the open door. He had no choice but to go around and close the thing. Once he was outside, he was drawn to the light inside the windows of the café, as surely as any man was ever drawn to a disaster of his own making. He needed to know what was going to happen, even if there was nothing he could do about it.

* * *

Amy Mitchell stopped chewing her gum and cleared her throat for a moment. It was still more dark than light outside, but the café opened early, and she wanted to get this over with. She stood rigid inside the main room, ignoring the nervous tickle that went up and down her spine. The door had opened behind her. Someone was standing there, but she wasn't going to turn around. She didn't care who saw her. People were going to find out sooner or later, anyway, that she was making some serious changes in her life.

"Care for a cup?" Linda Enger, the café owner, squinted as she walked over with her pot of coffee. She had a yellow kerchief tied around her curly, auburn hair and a white chef's apron covering her jeans and T-shirt. Red toenails peeked out of leather sandals and a big, diamond ring circled her wedding finger.

"No, no thank you." A light had burned

out overhead, and it was darker in this part of the café than elsewhere. Amy wasn't sure the other woman saw her well enough to recognize her, since dawn was barely starting to light up the sky.

Linda walked closer and finally cocked her head sideways a little. "Amy?"

She nodded. "I've come to see if you have a job."

"Oh." Linda blinked and then paused. "I haven't seen you in town for a long time. Is everything all right?"

Amy realized in a sudden burst of panic that she still had her gum in her mouth.

"Sorry," she said as she reached up and removed the gum. She always chewed a new stick of spearmint gum when she went out to do the chores. It helped with the smells in the barn. But she usually took it out as soon as she went back in the house. This morning she had been so upset, she'd forgotten.

"No problem," Linda said. "So it's a job, is it?"

Amy had an empty wrapper in her pocket, and she quietly folded it around the used gum while she nodded and tried to look competent for the other woman. "I am available for any shift you might need. I could do the cleaning, too. I'm good with a mop."

Amy stuffed the wrapped gum into her jacket pocket and rubbed her hands against the denim jeans she was wearing. She hadn't had a paying job before. Shoveling out the barn didn't count. She quickly glanced around. Two local ranch hands were at a far back table arguing about something, probably the price of wheat, but they were paying no attention to the front of the café.

"You have such a beautiful floor," Amy said, just to keep the conversation going. The black-and-white squares and vinyl-covered ruby chairs were part of a fifties look. "And I don't mind hard work."

"But what about your aunt?" Linda stepped over to the closest table and set the coffeepot down. "Doesn't she still need someone with her? I know her MS has been difficult on all of you."

Amy shifted her feet. "The doctor says she's well enough to be on her own more than she is." He'd been saying that for the last year, actually. It wasn't until twenty minutes ago that Amy had realized she was using her aunt's health as an excuse not to live her own life.

"That's good news," Linda said. "You're sure?"

"That's what he says. Sometimes the MS goes into remission for months—even years—and she's doing fine now. But I thought maybe—if I need to sometimes—I could take a break when business is slow and drive back to check on her. That is, if you have something for me."

Amy knew she shouldn't make any decisions about applying for a job when she was still angry. But she felt she had to do something right now to show she wasn't as pathetic as some people obviously thought. By people, she meant Shawn Garrett.

She had thought Shawn was her friend. But then she had also thought he had been joking when he had proposed she marry him to help him get more votes in his campaign for the state legislature. Shawn had always been a kidder, so she'd laughed and figured it was just his sense of humor—until this morning.

There had been no mistaking the bitter triumph in his voice as she'd stood in the hallway outside her aunt's kitchen and overheard him brag that Amy would gladly marry him once she read the article about Wade Stone being washed up after his latest injury on the rodeo circuit. Shawn must have paused to take a breath, because she'd then heard the rustle of a newspaper like he was pointing something out to her aunt. Then he'd muttered that it had been a year since the accident and so Wade was never coming back—

which meant Amy was wasting her time waiting for him.

Amy's blood pressure rose when she heard her aunt murmur in quiet agreement.

"Is something wrong?" Linda asked as she searched Amy's face.

"No, I'm doing fine." She forced her mind back to the café and looked at the other woman. "I was just thinking."

Amy's eyes narrowed all of a sudden. She wondered who else Shawn had been talking to about her feelings for Wade. She could bear many things, but she couldn't stand to have her neighbors gossip about her like she was some old spinster who pined away for a man who was beyond her reach—even though Shawn was right on one point. Wade had clearly forgotten anyone in Dry Creek existed, and that included her. She'd never received even a postcard from him in the nine years he'd been gone.

"You always seem like things are

good," Linda agreed, looking more relaxed. "I know it's been hard with your aunt, but—"

"She's not the problem." Amy tried to be fair. Her aunt had given up a career on Broadway to raise her after her parents had been killed in a car accident. "I want to do what I can for her. And my grandfather is around. He's not always—well, his mind drifts and he's not always quite there, but he'd be able to call for help if something was really wrong."

When she ran out of words, Amy just stood there.

Linda was silent as she studied her.

Please, God. Amy bit her lip as she prayed. *I need some help.*

"Well, I think we have a deal," the café owner finally said decisively. "My sister helps me until the middle of January, but she'll be going back to college then. So come back in a month or so. We could start you then."

"Oh." Amy swallowed.

Everything was quiet for a moment.

"That's not soon enough for you, is it?" Linda's smile faded. "I'm sorry. I just can't afford more help before then—it might be as late as February before I can start you. Things really pick up around here for Valentine's Day. But if I can swing it earlier, I'll let you know. In the meantime, let me fix you some breakfast. On the house. Free food is one of the perks of the job. That'll make you feel better."

"Thanks, but I've already eaten." Amy had to get back soon, or her aunt would worry about her. She just hoped Shawn was gone by then. She hadn't said anything to either of them. They could still be at the table, drinking tea and talking about her.

"Well, I'll be in touch then," Linda said as she turned to pick up the coffeepot from the table, where she had set it earlier. With that, the café owner started walking toward the men in the back, probably to refill their cups.

A soft footstep sounded behind Amy, but she didn't turn around. She knew she wore her disappointment on her face, and she had her pride. Life had been difficult for her—that was nothing new—but she was starting to feel helpless, and she didn't like that.

She had stayed home to care for her aunt, but she wanted to travel and see new places, too. Eventually, she hoped to have a husband and children. She wanted to raise her family in Dry Creek, but surely, Shawn wasn't her only choice.

Amy knew she should be turning to God for solace, but lately she found herself being angry with Him. Her resentment had been building for some time. God might be the Maker of heaven and earth, but He never seemed to care about her. She must be too small for Him to notice. First He'd taken her parents, and she'd gotten past that. Then He'd let the man she loved move away, and she was trying to cope. Now, it felt like He didn't care about her future at all.

Still, as angry as she was, she didn't want to broadcast her discontent. She didn't need anyone to see how discouraged she was and start a rumor that something was wrong with her. Shawn would be sure to throw in his two cents if he heard about it. Pride was all she had left, and she couldn't bear to look pathetic to people who'd known her since she was a child. So, it wouldn't hurt to stand still for a minute, until her face settled back into more peaceful lines.

"I've got a job for you." A woman's husky voice whispered behind her.

Amy almost recognized the voice, but she had to be wrong. She'd had this happen before in places far more public than the café. She'd hear one of the Stone family members, or so she'd think, and she'd be excited until she turned to face the person. Instead, it would be some stranger, and her heart would plummet. Usually, it was Wade who tripped her up, but his mother weighed on her heart, too.

She prepared herself for disappointment, but she turned around anyway, and there, in the open doorway, stood the one woman she wanted to see more than any other in the world—Gracie Stone.

"Oh, my," Amy whispered in surprise. The years rolled away, and she remembered how as a girl she'd run across the fields to the Stone house and Gracie would be waiting with a hug and a warm cookie for her. Gracie had been as much a mother to her as her aunt had ever been—maybe more.

Amy smiled. "I didn't know you were back."

Another shadow fell across the doorway, but Amy didn't have time for anyone else. Not when God was finally blessing her today by bringing back Gracie. She scarcely knew what to say, so she stood there grinning for a moment. "Are you staying at your ranch? I know it needs a lot of work, but—please say you're staying."

As much as she wanted to avoid any mention of Wade, she wanted to be near Gracie. God had known what she needed, after all.

"That's why I want to hire you," the other woman said, putting out her words one at a time as though she wasn't used to speaking. "I got here a couple of days ago and the house needs work. Mostly cleaning out the old cupboards. Washing things down. Maybe painting some walls."

"A couple of days ago? And you haven't stopped by?" Amy took a breath. She was surprised she hadn't noticed any lights in the old house. "Of course, I'll help." She felt herself relax. Now that Gracie was back, everything would be all right. "Aunt Tilly will be so happy to see you."

Finally, life would be what it was supposed to be.

The shadow in the doorway moved again. This time, Amy had to look. It was a man; she could see that from the shape of the Stetson on his head and the black silhouette he made against the grayness of the morning. If there were more bulbs in those light sockets on the porch, she might be able to see who it was.

Then he shifted slightly, and something about the nervous action reminded her of someone, but she couldn't remember who. Gracie was still talking.

"I was surprised Tilly never wrote to me when I was in—when I was away." Gracie finished what she was saying, her words halting. The questions in her eyes were directed at Amy. "I got letters from Mrs. Hargrove—she had a soft spot for me and the boys even before everything happened—but none from Tilly. I was worried about her."

"I'm sure my aunt meant to write. She hasn't been well, but I'm sure she would have written if she could."

Everything was silent for a moment, and Amy let herself remember. She hadn't realized it until now, but her aunt hadn't even mentioned the Stones after Gracie went away to prison. Amy had thought her aunt was just being sensitive to her heartbreak over Wade, but maybe it had been more than that. It was near that time her grandfather's dementia had started. Maybe her aunt was preoccupied with that. On several mornings, she had been pale and shaken after being up with him, unwilling to even talk about the night.

Gracie turned slightly, and the man in the shadows stepped forward. Amy gasped and then felt the blood drain from her face. She should have figured it out sooner. It was Wade Stone, taller and bigger than she remembered, but definitely him.

"Don't bother your aunt about us." His voice was flat. Under his hat, his black hair was long enough to touch the collar of his denim shirt. The shirt itself had been washed so many times that spots here and there had become faded, especially the tips of the collar, which lay open enough to show a white T-shirt underneath.

Amy had imagined this moment a thousand times after Wade had left without saying goodbye. At first, she had believed that the lack of a farewell was a wordless message to her that he was coming back for her. After all, he had kissed her in the moonlight outside of the church. He had said he would marry her and, even though she was only fifteen, she knew how the fairy tale went. She'd prayed earnestly and had been prepared to run away with him when he asked. He was her destiny.

Waiting for Wade to return, she'd turned down date after date in high school. She'd only gone to the prom because her aunt had bought her a dress that couldn't be returned and insisted she go. And then, by chance, Amy had read a news article in the *Billings Time,* telling all about the rodeo competitions Wade had won. Some woman with a glittery cowboy hat was kissing him as she gave him a tall, golden trophy. He had the crooked smile on his face that Amy knew so well, and he didn't look like he was missing her one little bit. He'd even been in Billings, so he wasn't far away; he could have come to see her. That's when she'd told God to ignore her prayers. She was tired of begging for a fantasy that was never going to come true, with a man who just didn't seem to care.

"Wade Stone," she finally found her voice enough to say with suitable coolness. "You're looking well. You must have recovered from your accident."

The one good thing about this morning was that Shawn's words had let her know Wade hadn't come back to Dry Creek because of any lingering affection for her. Even at this point in time, she might have grasped at the hope that he had and she would have felt foolish to be proven wrong, even if no one else had known her thoughts.

"I'm all right," he said gruffly.

His hat, a gray Stetson, hid the top part of his face, but she didn't need to see his familiar brown eyes to know he had changed. When she had known him, he was gangly and not yet a man. There was nothing boyish about him as he stood before her now though. His broad shoulders were squared. He looked powerful and a little wary, like a dog standing guard over some bone he'd just found. His legs were widely spaced, and his wool jacket open, a flashy, silver belt buckle with a rodeo scene all too visible. That must be one of his trophy belts.

"Good." She gave him a curt nod and forced herself to turn her attention to Gracie. "You have a job?"

She no sooner said the words than she realized she couldn't work for Wade's mother. Not if she wanted to avoid the pity of the gossips. She'd told Shawn more than she should have over the years, and he might not have told everyone about her crush on the man yet, but that didn't mean he'd keep silent if she went to work for the Stone family.

"I'm sorry," Wade murmured, his voice low and tense. She turned to him. For a second, it felt like all of the air rushed out of her. She suddenly wondered—was he really sorry? Was he going to apologize? For leaving her? For not coming back? Was God going to finally answer her prayers? Then Wade continued. "My mother shouldn't have offered you the job. It's a lot of work—hard physical work— and it's just not for you. You'd get dirty."

His face was weathered. A shadow of whiskers showed he hadn't shaved this morning, and his jaw was tense. When he stopped talking, his lips pressed too tightly together. He looked like something was bothering him, and he was ready to explode.

"I clean out *barns,*" she finally said.

He must not have heard that her family had gone through most of their money; after years of doctors' bills, they were no longer able to afford hired help of any kind for the ranch. If she didn't do it, it didn't get done. "Rakes. Wheelbarrows. Whatever. Dirt doesn't scare me."

She wasn't going to take the job, but she didn't want him to think it was because she was some kind of a princess. She'd learned a lot about work since he'd left and she took pride in being strong. Her fingernails were clipped short for a reason.

Wade opened his mouth like he was going to say more, but he was too late.

"I already told her she could have the job," Gracie said as she turned to her son. "I never go back on my word. The job is hers if she wants it."

"Thank you." Amy lifted her chin. At least one Stone family member had confidence in her. "Unfortunately, I won't be able to accept your kind offer." She shot a look at Wade. "But not because I'm afraid of getting a little dirt on my hands."

Wade grunted. "If it's not the dirt that bothers you, it must be working for the Stones that's the problem, is that it?"

He hadn't said the words loudly, but the force of them carried. The whole café went silent. The ranch hands stopped using their silverware. Linda had stopped walking, the coffeepot still in her hand. Amy could see everyone looking at them. She doubted even the poor lighting in the front of the café would disguise who they were.

Gracie finally gasped. "Wade—"

Amy looked him straight in the eye. She'd never seen him look so cold. "I'd be proud to work for your mother."

"But not me?" he asked with a twist to his mouth.

The chill in his manner didn't lessen any as he spoke. His eyes were almost black. Amy heard the sound of a chair pushing back, and one of the ranch hands rose to his feet, probably to help her if she needed it. Linda gestured for the man to sit back down.

Amy felt her cheeks burn. "I just—" She didn't remember Wade ever having this kind of an edge. She was suddenly unsure what to say. "I didn't say that. I—"

Wade waved away what was going to be an apology on her part. He ducked his head as if to shake off his feelings. "Forget about it. It's not a big deal. My mother would be the one you'd be working for, anyway. I'll stay clear of the house. I have enough to keep me busy outside."

Now, he looked defeated. Amy wondered how things had become so bad between them. He might not have come back to declare his undying love for her, but they had been friends at one time. She tried to meet his eyes again, but he was looking everywhere except at her.

"I'll take the job then—if that's okay," she said softly, changing her mind.

She never had been able to refuse the Stones anything. And Wade seemed troubled. Besides, she had been praying for years that he would come back, and maybe God had something to teach her now that he had. She'd figured out years ago that losing her parents had made her more vulnerable to the sorrow of good-byes than most people. Maybe if she spent some time around Wade she would be able to say farewell to him gracefully. Friend to friend. If she did that, she could get on with her life and not just pretend to do so.

Wade grunted and finally met her eyes. "Before we get started, you might as well know that I have one rule." He stopped to tip his hat back. "Anything you see or hear is off-limits. You're not to talk about what happens out at the ranch. Not to re-porters or anyone else."

An unexpected flash of anger swept through Amy. Did he think she was some kind of a groupie? "Of course I won't talk.

Besides, you might be some big man in the rodeo world, but not everyone around here is waiting for news about what you're going to do next."

"Me?" His eyes widened as he looked at her. She'd always liked his brown eyes, especially when they flashed golden like they were doing now. They turned to cat's eyes, flaring up with hot emotion. That's how his eyes had looked that night he kissed her.

"He's worried about me," Gracie interrupted quietly as she took a step closer to her son. "But I can't imagine anyone wants to know about me, either. Not after all this time."

"Oh, I wasn't thinking. Of course, I won't say anything," Amy assured them, feeling foolish. Now she was the one who couldn't look Wade in the eye. She'd never gossiped about Gracie at the time of the trial; she wasn't about to say anything now.

She never had believed Gracie was

guilty, anyway, not even after she heard her stand in front of the judge and confess that she had used a shovel to hit her husband on the back of the head while he sat on a bale of hay out by their barn. The courts had convicted her, even after everyone found out about the beatings and abuse, but Amy knew it wasn't right. Someone like Gracie would never have killed anyone, no matter what that person had done to her.

"See that you keep your word." Wade turned to walk out of the café.

Amy watched him go. By now, the sky was turning a rosy pink, and the light coming through the windows showed up everything in the café. For the first time since she'd realized it was Wade standing there, she remembered how she was dressed. She'd always pictured meeting him while she was wearing some sleek, black dress and high heels on her feet. She wanted to show him she'd turned into somebody. And make him regret not coming back for her.

But now—she looked down at her work clothes. She certainly had not made the kind of impression she had hoped. He wasn't likely to regret anything.

"I just wore my chore clothes this morning." Amy turned to Gracie and confessed, "I usually look better."

Gracie smiled. "Wade doesn't care what you're wearing."

Amy nodded. She supposed he didn't, at that. God must be trying to teach her something about the value of humility.

She followed Gracie to the open door, watching Wade all the time. His back was straight and strong as he walked slowly toward the pickups. His stride was a bit uneven, as though he was holding back a limp, but he seemed stiff rather than pained.

Suddenly, Amy noticed the bumper sticker on her vehicle and remembered—she needed to be sure Shawn didn't know

Wade was back. Shawn never had known when to keep his mouth shut, and she didn't want him saying anything to Wade about her waiting for him like some tragic figure in a soap opera. She was willing to try and put aside some of her pride, if that's what God intended for her, but she didn't want to be pitied.

"It's time we came back home," Gracie said as she put her arm around Amy. "It's God's goodness that we can be here."

"Yes," Amy agreed. She wondered if she should say something to Wade about Shawn's speculations. She had no idea what that would be, though. Maybe if she just treated Wade with the right touch of friendliness, absent any of the closeness she'd felt at one time, he wouldn't believe Shawn, even if the other man did say something about her waiting for Wade to come home. Surely, Wade would remember Shawn loved to tease.

She looked through the door at Wade and almost sighed. She'd reached down and pulled out her feelings for him years ago, like her emotions were tough weeds that wouldn't die unless the root was all gone. She wasn't sure if enough of her love for him was left inside her that it would develop into something, but she hoped not. She couldn't take the heart-break again.

Chapter Two

Wade breathed deep as he stood outside looking at Amy's red pickup. The paint had faded over the years, but the vehicle had been polished, and its silver chrome shone. The storm clouds had lifted, and the morning sun was finally here in all its Montana glory. Thankfully, the street was still quiet, and he took another determined breath. He didn't know what was wrong with him. Seeing Amy again had him off balance.

He hadn't felt so tongue-tied and awkward since he left Dry Creek. During his rodeo years, he'd gained a reputation for being able to hold his own with women. He hadn't dated much, but he'd had enough women say they were willing to go out with him that he knew he was doing something right. Being back here brought up his old insecurities, though, and made him feel like he was seventeen again.

He heard Amy and his mother walk out of the café, but he didn't turn around. Instead, he kept walking back to his pickup. It was then that he noticed there was a bumper sticker on the front of Amy's vehicle in addition to the one in the back. She must really plan to vote for that man.

"I didn't know you were so friendly with old man Garrett." He turned as he spoke. That made easy chitchat. It wasn't difficult to find something a woman was interested in and ask her about it. There was no reason for him to feel awkward.

Amy had her arm around his mother, but she stopped to look up at him.

"Don't worry. He might be running for

office, but he's not going to talk to the reporters, either." Amy lifted an eyebrow in what looked like annoyance.

Okay, so she'd been a little offended, Wade thought. He didn't blame her.

"It's not that." He nodded his head toward the bumper sticker. Maybe he needed a lighter approach. "I just wondered how the old man was doing."

"It's Shawn," Amy said, her lips pinching together.

Wade looked at her in astonishment. "*Our* Shawn?"

The years rolled away. He forgot about being easygoing as his mouth hung open.

"He's not *our* Shawn," Amy snapped. "He's just someone who wants to run for public office and—"

"Shawn Garrett?" Wade repeated. "The guy couldn't even get elected to the student council in high school. And I think he cheated in history. And math. Of course, he had to if he was going to pass anything. But the state legislature!"

The color was high on Amy's face, but it still took a moment for Wade to connect all of the dots. His heart sank. "You didn't get married to him or anything, did you?"

His eyes looked for her ring hand, but she had it around his mother's waist as they stood there. He should have checked for a ring earlier when they were inside. He'd forgotten that nine years had passed. She was likely married to someone; he was a fool to think otherwise. *But Shawn?*

"It's none of your business if I did," Amy said as she stepped away from his mother, stomped to her pickup and yanked the door open.

Amy was six inches shorter than Wade, yet somehow she managed to look down her nose at him as she stood by that open door like she was defending her pickup from him. "I'll come over to your house after I've stopped to let my aunt know where I am."

He shouldn't be grinning, but he was. There was no ring on her finger.

"You do that." Wade watched her swing herself up into the vehicle. She had always been graceful, and her shoulders moved smoothly with her arms as she settled herself behind the wheel.

He should have turned to go to his own pickup then, but he just stood there with his mother, both of them looking at that old, red Ford and Amy inside it. He didn't know what his mother was thinking, but he was having a hard time catching his breath. He just realized a ring wasn't a requirement anymore. Not all women were as tied to those gold bands as his mother was to hers. He didn't like thinking of Amy married to anyone. But wouldn't she have admitted the fact if she was married to Shawn?

"She's still as nice as ever," his mother said, glancing up at him with that look he was coming to recognize. Oh, no. She thought God was talking to her again.

Wade could only grunt. "It's not a sign, Mother. Seeing Amy like this."

"Oh, of course not, dear." She sounded innocent enough, even though he knew she wasn't being straight with him. She thought it was a sign, all right.

He needed to stop her matchmaking. "Amy's probably married to someone, even if it's not Shawn."

His mother grinned just like she had years ago when she caught him with his hand in the cookie jar. "She should be married. She's cute enough any man would be a fool not to marry her if he had a chance to make it happen—good-tempered, too."

He kept his mouth shut. There wasn't much he could add to that, anyway. His mother was right. Amy always had been sweet to everyone. He turned to walk away, and then he heard a grinding sound. He stopped and looked back. Amy was staring down at the wheel of her pickup or, more likely, the ignition. When the starter ground again, he began walking to her door. She had the window rolled down by the time he got close.

"It's not starting," she said.

"I see that."

By then, his mother had come over to the window, too.

"It's okay," his mother said. "You can ride back with us. Wade will come into town later and fix whatever's wrong with it. He's always been good at things like that."

Amy looked at him with indecision on her face.

"No need to spend money for someone else to fix it," he agreed. That old pickup of hers might be shined up nice on the outside, but he guessed the inside was held together with paper clips and baling wire. "I mean, money doesn't grow on trees around here."

Real smooth, he thought to himself as he tried to smile. Remind her that she's broke. What woman doesn't like that?

She frowned. "I can afford to pay you to repair it. Maybe not until after Christmas, but—"

"That's not what I meant. We're neighbors. Of course, I'll fix it. No charge."

"I'll pay. I've been saving some money to go back east for a visit, so I can use some of that."

"I see." He could hear that his voice sounded pinched and tinny. He cleared his throat, hoping to make it come out more normal, but then realized he had nothing to say. The tone of her voice made him think there was more to her words than she was saying. He wished he knew why she was going back east. Of course, he couldn't just ask, but he did remember that she had no relatives except the ones she lived with in Dry Creek, so if she was visiting back east, that probably meant she had a boyfriend somewhere. Maybe even someone she'd met on the internet.

"Be sure you meet in public places," he

said. "But not bars. Maybe a coffee shop. Or church. Church is good."

She looked at him like he was deranged.

"I mean, on your trip back east," he explained. "Be careful of strangers."

"I'm always careful," she said, her words clipped. "That's part of the problem. I haven't met a stranger in a long time."

"Well, that's good then." He hoped.

She didn't say anything to that so he cleared his throat and tried again. "Well, fortunately, I can probably fix what's wrong with your pickup. Most men could, so if there's someone—" He waited for her to fill in a name of a husband or boyfriend, but she didn't. "I'll just need to order a part for it."

She didn't protest, so he figured it was settled.

In less time than he would have thought possible, Amy was sitting beside him in his pickup. His mother had said her hip would be sore if she couldn't stretch her legs on the passenger side, so Amy had no choice but to slide in beside him.

He'd take what he could get when it came to being close to her. He was just glad he didn't have any crumpled chip wrappers on the floorboards and that his heater worked. A mile or two down the road, he managed to check Amy's neck to see if she had a ring hanging around it on a chain. The girls used to do that in high school. But she didn't have a necklace of any kind.

"Excuse me," he mumbled automatically. His elbow kept rubbing against her arm when he shifted gears. With the condition of the roads, he had already made his excuses more often than he liked. Added to that, he thought he caught the faint scent of spearmint. He would have asked her if she still chewed the gum, but she wasn't looking like she felt real friendly toward him. She probably thought he'd already asked too many questions.

His mother was doing fine with the conversation, anyway, going on about how she wanted to decorate their old house for Christmas and needed to buy some ornaments, since they didn't have any.

Wade felt Amy's every move, but she clearly wasn't as bothered as he was by the contact. He had never known a scratchy, wool jacket could be so tempting, though, especially after he noticed there wasn't even a tan line where she used to wear a ring. That meant she must not be divorced or anything like that, either.

"Sorry again," he repeated. This time, she was the one moving her arm, and she was doing it more than anyone needed to in his opinion. Not that he minded the contact; it's just that he could do without the memories that were coming back.

Feeling her elbow graze his arm reminded him of the freckles on the back of her hand. When she was twelve, she'd worn a bandage over them one whole summer because she was afraid they were going to spread to the rest of her body. He'd secretly hoped they would, but he hadn't said that to her because she had been so stricken by the thought.

He stole a glance at her now. Since she'd climbed in the pickup, she'd pulled the collar of that gray work coat closer and closer around her neck. But he didn't see any freckles anywhere. Just the smooth, creamy skin along the side of her face.

"I was just pointing out the new fence along the Garrett place to your mother." Amy turned and frowned at him.

He nodded, wondering if she could still read him like she used to be able to. Her expression certainly indicated she disapproved of something.

"I thought you would both be interested since you mentioned Shawn," she added a little primly.

Wade grunted. The sun was completely up by now, and there were no shadows to hide the expression on anyone's face, so he kept his eyes straight ahead. "I don't care about Shawn one way or the other. I was just surprised. That's all."

He'd figured out by now that Shawn's name was coming up in the conversation more than would be normal if he didn't mean something to Amy. Why else would she point out those white-and-red cardboard signs nailed to that new fence begging folks to vote for the guy?

"Guess I'll have to register to vote," Wade added, trying his best to be pleasant about it. Men saw their childhood sweethearts get married to other men every day. Young love didn't last for most people.

Maybe he'd even come back to cast his ballot for Shawn, if he could. Voting wasn't the sort of thing a man who lived in hotels had to worry about. Of course, it was a whole lot of months before any election. One thing he'd have to say for Shawn—the man was smart enough to know he'd need an early start to collect enough votes to win.

It didn't take many fence posts for Wade to remember everything he knew about the Garrett ranch. His father had complained bitterly about the fifteen hundred head of purebred Angus cattle old man Garrett ran on his place. And he had only one son to help him—a sickly boy who came in last every time the kids raced at school. The Stone family had worked to manage eighty head of scrub cattle in their best years, but, as often as not, Wade's father would get drunk and let the cattle into the wrong pasture or decide they needed to head down the road somewhere, so he'd open a fence gate.

Wade and his brothers, all of them sturdy boys, had a hard time fixing all their father did wrong, and yet the man made them feel that Shawn Garrett was worth more as a son than the three of them added together. It was Tyler or Jake who had decided to call Shawn "that puny boy," but they'd all been jealous of him.

"There's nothing wrong with being a civil servant," Amy said a bit later, eyeing him like she didn't trust his response.

Wade nodded. He supposed he'd get used to being polite even when he felt like ripping the man's heart out. "Of course not. Lincoln. Washington. All those guys."

"Well, maybe that's not quite Shawn," Amy admitted wearily.

She didn't seem to have anything more to say, and for once, she was keeping her arms quietly at her side.

"Oh—" his mother said suddenly from her place by the passenger window. "I forgot to get the eggs!"

Wade slowed his pickup to a stop. They were twelve miles outside of town by now. It wouldn't take long to drive back, but the quiet of the dawn was over. People would be up and around. He trusted Linda at the café not to say anything about them, and the ranch hands probably didn't know who they were. But if other people saw him and his mother, they would start talking. And then the rumors would start to grow. He wasn't sure either one of them was ready for that.

"We have eggs," Amy said. "Stop at our place, and I'll run in and get you a few."

"Oh, would you?" his mother said, her face lighting up again. "They're for Wade's sausage-and-egg scramble."

"I told you I don't need breakfast," he said.

Amy finally turned to him, her eyes blazing. "Of course you need breakfast. It's the most important meal of the day. Your mother is doing her best for you. Which you would know if it ever occurred to you to make *her* breakfast for a change."

Wade felt his world tilt on its axis. He and Amy had been a little testy with each other back in the café, and maybe she could sense he wasn't happy about her and Shawn, but the Amy he had known never really scolded anyone—not like this. She was sweet and forgiving and much too good for anyone. She might look faint when he kissed her and swing her elbows all around in the pickup, but she would never criticize him or con- tradict him—at least not like this. She'd been a good church girl. She prayed. She sang in the choir. She never said anything bad about anyone. Now that he thought about it, he should have seen that she had changed when she made such a big deal about refusing to work for him.

"And not just a cold-cereal breakfast either," Amy continued, gesturing with her hands. The collar of her jacket had fallen away, and he saw the pulse in her throat. "I mean a real breakfast. You probably don't even know how to cook eggs or oatmeal or anything like that."

He tried to keep his tone mild. "I usu- ally eat fortified cereal. Comes from a box. With raisins and cranberries and nuts—almonds. It has all the vitamins a body needs."

Amy gave a small sound of disgust, whether at him or the cereal, he wasn't sure.

"Well," she continued, looking down at her hands like she was already regretting her outburst. "If your mother wants to make some kind of a scramble for you, I aim to see she has the eggs to do it."

"Fine." Wade gave up. "Fine. I was just trying to save her the bother."

"Maybe I should make crepes instead," his mother said, turning to Amy with a sympathetic twinkle in her eyes. "I heard from Mrs. Hargrove a few years ago that you had sent away for a correspondence course in French cooking. Maybe you could help me learn how to make them. I've always thought they were so elegant."

"I'd love to," Amy said, looking back up and beaming at his mother with the old enthusiasm she used to direct toward him.

"They were the first thing we learned to make."

"The way to a man's heart is through his stomach," his mother said complacently. "Wade here likes French food."

"I do?" As near as he could remember, he wasn't much on foreign food of any kind. Beef and potatoes were more his style.

"Of course you do," his mother said as she gave him a look that said he better not contradict her. "You don't want her to cook for Shawn. Didn't you set a bag of that French coffee on the shelf in the enclosed porch this morning? Where I have the coffeepot rigged up?"

His mother had certainly learned to be a lot more direct while she'd been in prison. He wasn't sure he was ready for it. "That's French-roasted. I don't think it qualifies as French food. Besides, I would have gotten the plain-roasted if I'd been able to find it when I stopped in Miles City."

"You don't need to worry," Amy said, giving him a look that said he better not give anything his mother was saying another thought. "I'm teaching her—that's all. There will be no cooking from me. Not for you or Shawn, either one."

Wade heard her words, but something still wasn't right. She was wound up tight. Many years might have passed, and she might be annoyed with him, but he could still read her feelings.

He looked over at her. "Why are you so touchy about Shawn Garrett anyway? What'd he do to you?"

Amy turned to look at him, and her eyes spit more fire than he wanted to see. "He asked me to marry him. That's what the fool did. And he told my aunt about it, and now she thinks I should, too."

With that, she burst into tears. Wade didn't worry anymore about trying to appear smooth. He parked the pickup on the side of the road, reached over and drew her to him. He felt like some befuddled knight of old, ready to slay the dragon, if he could only see it. This was his Amy in tears. He'd expected her to marry someone, but he thought the man would be the prince of some small country or maybe an opera singer at the Metropolitan. He never considered it might be puny boy, Shawn Garrett.

He looked up to see a satisfied smile on his mother's face. He shook his head at her, hoping she wouldn't say anything. She nodded like she understood, and it was silent in the cab, except for the soft hiccups coming from Amy's rosebud mouth.

Amy was appalled with her tears. She never cried, but when she did, the hiccups always followed. Fortunately, everyone knew where the Mitchell ranch was, so she didn't need to tell Wade how to get there. He still had his arm loosely around her as he used one hand to drive up the short dirt road to her grandfather's house.

Wade's arm was distracting enough; she didn't need to risk further tears or hiccups by trying to explain anything to him.

"It wasn't a real proposal." That much finally burst out of her as they got close enough to the house so that Wade could park. She took a deep breath and looked around, trying to focus. She was glad it was winter so no one could see that the weeds needed cutting back around the lilac bushes. Or that the barn needed a new foundation.

"It's all right." Wade patted her shoulder as he pulled the key out of the ignition.

Even Gracie put a gentle hand on her knee. "Don't worry."

Amy looked back and forth between the concerned faces of Wade and his mother. "I'm fine. Really. Shawn just meant it as a joke. About his campaign. Shawn isn't— I mean, that's not it—"

"A man should never joke about a proposal," Gracie said, her lips firm.

"No, with Shawn, it's okay," Amy said. "Really."

They were all silent a minute, and then Wade opened the driver's door and started to slide out. He looked at Amy like he was wondering why she hadn't moved to follow him.

"I'll go out your mother's door," she said, in case that was his problem.

"Oh, there's no need for me to go inside, dear," Gracie said with a slight smile that puzzled Amy until she heard the rest of what the woman had to say. "I'll just sit here. You and Wade go ahead. You young people need some time alone. We old people just get in the way."

"You're not old! And—" Amy protested, but Gracie handed her the metal bowl for the eggs.

"You can come this way," Wade added as he finished getting out of the pickup.

Once he was on the ground, he even held a hand out to help her move past the gear shift. Then, when she was ready to step down, he held his arms up and lifted her down as though she were an invalid. Or a china doll.

"We don't need any time alone," she said when her feet were on the ground. "Don't worry about your mother. She's just—"

She glanced up in time to see his lips tighten. He moved back, pulling her sideways with him so that they were no longer in the space left by the open door. Instead, her back rested on the frame of the pickup. His mother couldn't see them.

"Is that Spearmint gum I smell?" he asked with a little bit of a smile curving his lips as he kept looking at her. He held out his hand for the bowl, and she gave it to him. He set it back inside the pickup.

The day was warmer than it had been, but she could still see her breath with each word. And the wind was blowing. "I don't know why I cried."

"Shawn has me to answer to if he doesn't treat you right." Wade brushed some strands of loose hair away from her cheeks and then left his hands there to cup her face. "He might joke around some, but he should know better than to upset you."

"Yes, well…" Amy murmured. No man had ever upset her as much as Wade, but she couldn't find the words to say so. Not when he was looking at her like he was ready to do battle on her behalf.

"It's not Shawn's fault. I'm sure he'll make a fine husband. He just needs to settle down," she said, trying to be fair to the other man.

That only made Wade press his lips closer together. His eyes grew tawny and one of his thumbs moved to caress her jaw, making her shiver where he touched her.

She thought for a moment that he was going to kiss her, and her heart almost stopped from the wonder of it—or maybe the terror of it, she wasn't sure. She'd never recovered from their one kiss all those years ago.

Then his eyes changed. His hands dropped down to his sides, and he stepped back.

"We better go get those eggs." He reached back into the pickup to get the bowl.

She could only nod. Her heart started back up again, and she took a deep breath.

The wind seemed colder than it was before. She started to walk toward her family's house. Wade followed behind her.

When they were almost to the front steps, her grandfather opened the door. He usually sat in his recliner by the television all day, but he must have looked out the window as they drove up. She wished he'd combed his hair, but white tufts stuck out from his balding head. The black suspenders he wore held his jeans in place, and he'd obviously forgotten again where his clean shirts were. He was wearing a thin undershirt that she recognized from the rag bag she kept under the kitchen sink. He held something behind his leg, and she assumed it was the steel cane he sometimes used.

"Is that the Stone boy with you?" He scowled as she and Wade started to climb the steps.

"Yes," she murmured, a little surprised. Her grandfather didn't recognize many neighbors anymore. Or, if he did, he confused their names with people on the television shows he watched.

Then her grandfather moved quicker than he had in years and pulled the old BB gun out from behind him. He pointed it at Wade. "I don't want any of you Stone men messing around my girls. Not anymore. No siree. You're trouble, you are, and I won't stand for it. I saw you out there by the pickup."

Her grandfather wobbled, and the gun moved back and forth until it was pointed at her. Wade moved quickly, standing in front of her, alarmingly close to the gun.

"I mean no harm," Wade said cautiously. "Just bringing Amy home."

She gasped as she tried to move around Wade, but he gripped her arm preventing her.

"'We're just here to get some eggs," she said.

She was pretty sure that gun wasn't loaded, but she didn't want to take any chances. "Set the gun down, Grandpa. What television show do you have on anyway?"

Maybe this time, he had gotten the names right and the story wrong.

"There's nothing worth watching this early in the morning," her grandfather complained, but he lowered the gun, and the fire went out of him.

Amy felt Wade's grip lessen on her arm. She didn't know how she was ever going to explain what had just happened. She remembered how proud her grandfather used to be. He'd be mortified if the neighbors knew how confused he was these days.

"Are you ever going to fix me breakfast?" her grandfather complained, sounding even more peevish than usual. "I'm hungry."

"I'll get you something to eat just as soon as I get some eggs for Gracie," Amy said, trying to soothe the old man. He was seldom up in time to join her and her aunt for breakfast.

With that, her grandfather turned and stepped back inside, leaving the door to the house open.

"It isn't always like this," Amy whispered as she walked with Wade into the place where she'd been raised. He'd been inside her house before, but not many times. Usually, she was the one who escaped over to the Stone place. Aunt Tilly was very particular about spotless floors, and she and Wade had always had mud or dried grass on their shoes after they had tramped through the coulee that ran along the south border of their two ranches.

Amy was barely inside before she heard the voice of her aunt calling from the kitchen. "Amy, is that you? What's going on out there?"

With that, her grandfather pointed the remote at the television and turned it on. "Time for *Gunsmoke*."

The sounds of hoofbeats filled the living room.

"Turn it down, Grandpa," Amy said as she glanced back up at Wade. "I'm sorry about all this."

"You could use some help," Wade said behind her as she started to walk toward the kitchen.

She turned and gave him a slight smile. "I'm fine. Please, make yourself at home. I won't be a minute. Give me the bowl and have a seat."

He handed her the bowl, and she watched until he sat down on the straight-back chair next to the door he'd just come through. It wasn't the most comfortable chair in the living room.

"Amy?" Her aunt's voice came from the kitchen again.

"I'll be right back," Amy said as she went to see what was wrong.

The winter light came from the east side of the house, so the kitchen table sat in front of that window like it had for several generations. Over time, the sun had lightened the wood, but her aunt still kept it uncovered. She was sitting there now, resting her morning coffee cup on a glass coaster and looking at the *Billings Time* which was spread out in front of her. Surely, it wasn't the newspaper that had the article Shawn was looking at earlier. It looked like it was mostly grocery ads.

"Shawn's gone?" Amy asked as she walked closer to the table. His cup was still sitting there, but it was empty. A plate with some muffin crumbs sat nearby. She supposed she should be glad he'd taken his newspaper with him.

"Where were you?" her aunt asked, looking up. She wore a red, plaid robe, gathered up tight around her throat, and pink, rubber-tipped curlers in her dyed-brown hair. She'd scrubbed her face, though, and wore a trace of mauve lipstick and some mascara to give herself color. Even at her sickest, Aunt Tilly insisted a woman needed lipstick and mascara.

Her aunt's eyes were accusatory as she looked at Amy. "Shawn wanted to say goodbye to you. He even looked for you out in the barn to see if you were still doing chores, but then he saw that the pickup was gone. You need to be nicer to Shawn. That boy has a future."

"I had an errand to run."

"He's not out there, is he?" her aunt demanded as she jerked her head toward the living room. "I heard voices and—"

"No, it's not Shawn." Amy walked over and opened the door of the refrigerator. The eggs she'd gathered this morning were still in the bucket she'd left in the hall, but the eggs from yesterday were washed and neatly arranged in a carton on the middle shelf. She opened the carton and pulled out enough eggs to fill the metal bowl. "You'll never believe who is back though—"

Amy turned around just in time to see her aunt's face grow pale.

"What's wrong?" Amy asked.

"Don't tell me it's one of those Stones." Her aunt was so upset she practically hissed the words. "I thought I heard Grandpa say the name, but I didn't believe it was possible."

Amy held the bowl of eggs very still. "Do you feel all right?"

She stepped over to the counter to set down the bowl, then walked over to her aunt and pressed her hand to the older woman's forehead. "You're not warm."

"I'm not sick. Answer me, child. Is it one of the Stones out there?"

Her aunt's temperature might be normal,

but something was wrong. "Yes, it's Wade. He's here because Gracie moved back home. I'm going to help her get her place put back to rights, but he's not staying. The paying job is with her."

"You're not to have anything to do with either one of them." Her aunt bit down on each word until a tiny vein started to throb on her forehead. "Do you hear me? Nothing. We're not that desperate for money. I don't know what they are thinking, anyway. They never should have come back here."

"Of course they should come back." Amy stepped away from her aunt. "This is their home. I mean, at least Gracie—"

"They'll murder you in your sleep over there." Her aunt's voice rose until it was shrill.

"I'm not sleeping there." Amy's tone went higher, too. "And you're forgetting they're our neighbors. Neighbors help each other around here. You always said that."

The sound of the television grew louder in the living room. There must be a battle on *Gunsmoke.*

"I'm not forgetting anything." Aunt Tilly turned her head away from Amy and said much more quietly, "You need to stay away from them—that's all. Please. Trust me on this."

Amy was silent for a moment. Maybe her aunt had been so sick she'd forgotten the friendship she'd had with the Stones. "You used to go out on the porch and wave to them every evening around chore time. And someone in the family would always wave back. Not just the kids, either. Mr. Stone waved sometimes, too. I was so surprised he would. I think they used to wait for you. I know you used to look forward to it."

"That was a long time ago. And too many things have gone wrong."

Her aunt still wouldn't look at her.

"Gracie's the same person," Amy finally said. "She served her time. I'm taking her out some eggs, and then I'll come back and fix Grandpa's breakfast. But then I'm going over to help her get settled in her home again."

Amy had never defied Aunt Tilly before. Not like this.

"Sometimes, things happen." Her aunt kept talking. She'd closed her eyes and seemed to be muttering to herself. "Things that just can't be undone."

Everything was quiet for a minute, even the television in the other room.

"I'll be back soon," Amy said as she went over and picked up the bowl of eggs. There was no point in answering any accusations right now. Not when Gracie was waiting.

When Amy stepped into the living room, she saw her grandfather staring at the picture of the streets of old Dodge City on the television. But there was no Wade.

Then she saw him through the small, square window in the front door. He was waiting outside. The knot inside her stomach eased up. If he'd been waiting on the porch, he wouldn't have heard her aunt say those things about his family. She knew her aunt didn't really mean them. The older woman had just been surprised; that's all. The Stones had always been their friends.

Amy opened the door, and Wade turned to look at her.

His face held no warmth. She wondered if she had imagined that he had almost kissed her earlier.

"It's not so cold anymore." She tried to sound cheerful as she stepped outside.

He nodded. "Seems that way."

He stood and looked at her for a minute, and she glanced along the side of the house. The kitchen window was closed. He couldn't have heard anything if he was standing where he was. The ground was frozen beside the house, but there was enough frost to see if anyone had stepped off the porch for any reason. There were no footsteps.

She hesitated, but then decided she couldn't apologize for what he hadn't heard, at least not without telling him what her aunt had said. There was nothing to do but walk with him over to his pickup, so she did.

She smiled as Gracie rolled down her window. Then Amy handed the bowl up through the opening. "If I had a bigger bowl, I'd give you more eggs."

"Oh, these are fine." Gracie looked down, and her lips curved. "Brown eggs. I haven't had a brown egg in years. I used to raise Island Red Hens just for their eggs. They're lovely birds."

"That's what I have, too." Amy stepped back from the pickup. "You'll like their eggs—everyone does. Of course, you already know that. I have a few things I need to do here, and then I'll walk over to your place."

"Oh, but you can't walk. That's too far," Gracie protested.

Amy just shook her head. "I used to do it all the time, remember? And when I didn't walk, I ran. The exercise will be good for me."

"But that was summer—" Gracie said again, her distress obvious. "It's cold out now, and there's still some snow—"

"It's warming up. I'll be fine." Amy was suddenly aware that all of the concern had come from Gracie. Wade didn't even look like he was surprised she wasn't coming with them. Maybe he had heard the conversation in the kitchen, after all. His eyes sure didn't have that soft look in them that they'd had only a few minutes ago. "I just need to do a few things with my aunt first. I think she's— I need to call the doctor and see if her medications are off somehow. She's hasn't been acting like herself. Gets upset easily, and she never used to do that. Says things she doesn't mean."

She was hoping that if Wade had heard what her aunt had said, maybe those words would make it better.

"Oh, I hope there's nothing wrong with Tilly." Gracie set the bowl of eggs down on the seat and reached for the door handle. "Maybe I should go in and—"

"No," Wade interrupted her abruptly and started walking around to the other door of the pickup. "We don't have time to stay." He reached the other side of the pickup and opened his door. "We need to get home."

"But—" Gracie protested.

Wade shut the pickup door as he settled himself behind the wheel.

He turned to his mother. "Tilly will be fine once we're gone. Don't worry about her."

Amy's heart sank. He had heard what her aunt had said. She wished she knew what to say to make it all better, but she didn't.

Wade was starting his engine. There

was nothing else to do but step back so he could turn his pickup around and head back to the main road. Amy owed him an apology. Hopefully, by the time she saw him next, she would have some idea of what was wrong with her aunt and could give a reasonable explanation for her rudeness.

Amy crossed her arms as she watched the Stone pickup make its way down the lane that would lead them home, but she wasn't ready to go back inside yet. Something was deeply wrong around here.

She looked at her grandfather's house, seeing it as a stranger might. The white paint on the place was chipped in places. She'd meant to scrape off the old paint and add new paint this past summer, but there hadn't been enough time, not after she'd finished planting the field behind the barn with wheat. They didn't have any cattle left, but the money she made from the sale of the wheat paid the taxes for the year, so she had to do that first. Taxes on farmland weren't cheap, and she wished money wasn't so tight. Her grandfather refused to lease the rest of the land to anyone, saying he didn't trust them. Her egg money kept them in groceries, and her grandfather got a small social security check that they used for utilities, but her aunt hadn't worked long enough to qualify for any benefits.

For the first time ever, when looking at her home, Amy clearly saw it as it was. A once-proud house that was slowly falling apart. She used to be pleased with everything about her family, both the place where they lived and the way they lived. Her grandfather and aunt had always been good, decent people. But something had changed inside of them. Bitterness filled the house now—and a certain smallness of heart when it came to others.

She wasn't sure she understood it.

She feared the problem was that her grandfather couldn't work any longer, and he was frustrated—both with himself and with her. She didn't know how to do everything that needed to be done around the ranch. He'd said more than once over the last few years that he wished he'd had a son instead of daughters. They couldn't afford to pay anyone to do the things that should be done, and her grandfather refused to let her ask for help. So she did her best, but she couldn't do all a man could—especially not with the housework added.

And, of course, there was her aunt's illness. The doctor said she was in remission, but her aunt didn't seem to care. She lived like she was an invalid, spending the days in her robe and not going out, even though the doctor said she could. She seemed shriveled and afraid.

Amy wondered if anyone else in the house realized how much work it took just to keep the place going.

"Amy." Her grandfather opened the door again and looked out. "What's keeping you? I still haven't had my breakfast."

"I'll be right there." She might not understand her relatives, but they were the only family she had, and she owed them for taking her in when she had been orphaned as a child. Both her aunt and grandfather had open hearts back then.

And they would again, if she had anything to do with it. Maybe her feeling that life was passing her by wasn't her most important problem. It wasn't that she wanted to leave this community, it's that she wanted to leave the feelings in this house. Her soul was shriveling here. Maybe she needed to pray that God would help her family love their neighbors again. That might make her feel like she was living the life in front of her more fully.

She decided to add their family to the prayer chain at church. She wouldn't need to say what was wrong, but if everyone prayed, God would surely help them.

She hadn't taken two steps into the house before she heard Aunt Tilly on the telephone, talking low and serious to someone. Her aunt sounded scared. Amy felt some relief. Maybe that was the problem. If it was fear that was the stumbling block preventing her aunt from welcoming Wade and his mother home, then all Amy needed to do was to help her family understand that the Stones weren't going to hurt anyone.

After spending a few minutes with the Stones, Amy knew they weren't a threat to anyone. She took a deep breath and bowed her head. In time everything would be back to what it had been years ago. It had to be. She couldn't bear to imagine it any other way.

"Please, God," she added in a whisper. *"Help us all."*

Chapter Three

The drive down the dirt lane to their house had too many bumps and wasn't long enough to calm Wade. He still felt the stress in his shoulders after clenching his fists as he sat there listening to Amy's aunt talk about him and his mother like they were—what?—criminals at best, madmen at worst.

He took a breath and reminded himself that he had expected this to happen.

He parked his pickup beside the back porch and sat there, looking straight ahead. Who was he kidding? The truth was he might have expected that behavior from some of the people in Dry Creek, but not from the Mitchells.

They were the neighbors they could see from their house. They were the closest people they'd had to friends. They'd turned to them for help when needed and had felt bound to help them in return. Even his father had understood that and treated them well. The two families had always been neighbors in the truest sense of the word. He hoped his mother never knew Amy's family was set against them now.

He heard a noise and turned to his mother.

"Wait," Wade said, but she had already opened her door. "The ground is still icy. Give me a minute and—"

He was too late to help her. She had left the bowl of eggs on the seat for him to carry, and she was already climbing out. Then she was standing on the frozen ground, looking back at him through her open door.

"The ice is why we can't let Amy walk over here," she scolded him as she stood there. The wind had added color to her cheeks and was blowing strands of her black hair around. "I'm going to go inside and watch from the window. When she starts out, you'll need to go get her."

"Just let me come around and help you." Wade balanced the bowl in his hands as he stepped out. Then he rounded the back of his pickup and offered his arm to his mother. "Don't worry. Amy will be fine."

"She could fall and break a leg out there."

Wade kept silent, making sure his mother held on to him. He didn't have much experience with love and, outside of Amy, hadn't felt the need to protect anyone in a long time. But the gentleness he felt for his mother almost overwhelmed him as he led her to the house.

She was fragile and precious. And worried about those eggs he carried like they were the only ones left on earth.

He didn't want her watching for Amy, not when his childhood friend wasn't likely to show up. And, as much as it might sting, he knew Amy was right to forget about them. Her family was opposed to her being with any of the Stones, and he had never known Amy to defy either her aunt or her grandfather. Wade might not have any future with her, but he didn't want to be the cause of discord in her life.

"I could hire someone from Miles City to come." Wade stepped up to the enclosed porch and gestured for his mother to go ahead of him. He let the door slam behind him as he went inside, too. This room had a solid wall on the north and partial screens on all the other sides. Wind blew through here, but it did give some shelter and his mother kept a few of her things out here.

"But Miles City is too far away," his mother protested. "Whoever you get will be a stranger."

Wade didn't answer as he opened the door which led into the main part of the house. He didn't blame his mother. Amy accepted her and someone else might not. Besides, Amy was sweet. He wondered if he really had smelled spearmint gum on her breath this morning or if his memories were simply rising up to haunt him.

The truth was, he realized with a stab, that his whole view of Amy might be nothing but memories. She'd been a girl back then, and her opinions on life were unspoiled by the experiences of the last years. She could be a completely different person now.

"Let's get you inside," Wade muttered as he led his mother into the kitchen.

The thought Amy had changed set him back some. But the sun shone bright as they stepped inside, and he was determined to be upbeat. After one look around, he knew he'd need it for the tasks ahead.

It had been dark this morning when

they'd left and, even with the flashlight, last night he hadn't really seen how bad everything looked. Over the years, dust and dead flies had blown into the corners. The broken dish he'd seen last night was a white plate of some kind, and the pieces were scattered around. It looked like a bird had built a nest on the shelf above the refrigerator some years ago and then abandoned it.

"We can't let Amy see our place like this," Gracie announced as though she were seeing the kitchen for the first time, too.

She paused and then shook her head. "I told myself I needed to rest for a few days before I tackled everything, but with all this dirt in here how can I be out there in the barn sleeping the day away?"

"Are you feeling okay?" Wade asked in alarm. His mother never slept in the middle of the day. She barely sat down.

She nodded her head. "It's just been so nice to have everything quiet so I can sleep. That's what I missed most in— Well, when I was gone."

She looked away from him, so he couldn't see her face, but she continued in a small voice. "There was no peace there, just noise and more noise. And all metal sounds, no birds or anything. That's what I hated. There is never any pure silence in a place like that—not even in the middle of the night."

Wade nodded. He felt bad for what she'd been through, but sympathy would only make her feel worse. So he cleared his throat. "It might be quiet out in the barn, but it's cold, too. The furnace in here should still work well enough that we can heat the house."

Wade set the bowl of eggs on the old tile counter. "I could fix up a place in one of the bedrooms upstairs for you. I'm sure all the beds and mattresses are still there."

They had left everything as it was when his mother went to prison. His father's ancestors had built the house when they proved up on their homestead almost a century ago, and there was furniture in the attic from past generations. There hadn't been a mortgage on the place for decades, and no one thought of selling the place, not even with all of its sagging floors and uneven wallboards.

"I had a double bed in my old room," Wade said. It had been his reward for being the oldest son, and the tallest. His two brothers had shared a room.

"I'm fine with the bedroom down-stairs."

"But—" He stopped almost as soon as he started. Then, into the silence, he asked, "Isn't that the room you shared with dad?"

His mother nodded. "It always gets the morning light."

She turned to him and smiled. "When there was a full moon, I used to stand by the window and look out on the yard. At midnight, everything looked like it was edged with silver. I missed that—not even knowing if the moon was full or not. The days didn't seem right."

Wade nodded. His mother had enough of her Cherokee spirit left to miss the sky and the moon. And the quiet of the wind-swept prairie that made up this part of Montana.

"But before we do anything, I'd like us to fix up the kitchen," his mother said. "That's the heart of a home. I'll have Amy start in here with the paint." She paused to look around again. "Maybe I'll go with a light green. I just wish we hadn't let everything go to ruin."

Wade felt a stab of guilt. "I should have come back and seen to things, but—" He stopped to take a breath and then forged ahead. "There's no excuse. I should have. That's all."

"You were living your own life. That's all you needed to be doing."

"Well—" he forced a cheer into his voice that he didn't feel "—I wouldn't worry about how things look now. We'll get it all back in shape before anyone notices."

He tried to see everything through the eyes of a stranger. The propane stove his mother used for cooking now was on the enclosed porch, but she kept what food she had inside the house. A few cans of soup and one of tuna fish, along with a clear glass bowl, sat beside the sink. An unopened box of wheat crackers lay beside the cans. He noted that she had shoved the old metal cooler into a far corner before they left this morning.

"It's just common courtesy to mop the floor before she gets here," his mother said and then frowned.

Wade noticed where her eyes were looking. Gray stains lined one side of the floor where rain and snow had gotten in over the years. He figured there would be mold under the linoleum there, but he couldn't do much about it right now.

"I don't think we need to stand on

courtesy today," Wade muttered without thinking and then wished he could pull the words back. He walked over and grabbed the broom from its hanger behind the door to try and distract her from his words. "I'll make quick work of the dust at least."

"What do you mean? We don't need to stand on courtesy?" His mother stood with her hands on her hips, studying him. "People need their neighbors in this kind of country. We always use our best manners when we're around those who live close by."

"I can't argue with that." Wade started sweeping. They'd do better to adopt a rattlesnake or two as neighbors, but he didn't need to tell his mother that. "And you did teach me manners. I just don't always use them."

His mother was quiet for a minute.

"She's not really interested in Shawn, you know," she finally said, sympathy in her voice.

He was almost relieved that his mother thought that was the problem.

"It doesn't matter," he said as he finished the sweeping. The broom had picked up most of the bits of things that had been scattered, even the pieces of glass.

His mother wasn't done with him, though. She must have been waiting for him to look up from the floor.

"Of course it matters," she said patiently. "You and Amy were always close. You can be again."

Wade shook his head. "I don't think so."

He leaned on the broom for a minute. "And it's probably for the best. Things change. People change."

"Things don't change that much," his mother said to him. "Not things of the heart."

He didn't know how to begin to tell her how wrong she was. She should know things changed—all the time.

"Why do you still wear his ring?" he asked.

She was silent for so long, he thought she wasn't going to answer. Then she whispered, "I used to love him. He was my husband."

The pain in her voice made Wade wince. "Sorry. I shouldn't have said anything."

"It's all right," she said. But then she turned to face the cupboards and started opening doors like she was looking for something she couldn't find.

He stood there for a minute, listening to his mother move things around and wondered if she was just doing it so that she could steady herself and not look at him.

The least he could do was to give her room to grieve the past. He walked over to the corner farthest from her.

"I wonder how that rock ever got to be in here," he said as he squatted down. A change of topic was what they needed, and the rock certainly gave it to them.

It was too large to be a pebble and not nearly big enough to be a useful rock. But there it sat, under the edge of the cabinet, next to the stove. He'd thrown enough rocks as a boy to know this one was the perfect size for it.

Wade looked at the broken window in the kitchen. None of the other windows in the house were even cracked. "Someone tossed this in here—deliberately."

Wade picked up the rock, even though he knew there would be no clues as to who had thrown it. The mess it left behind could tell him something, though. "That window must have been broken years ago for all these leaves and twigs to get in here. And the damp."

"It was probably just some boys," his mother said as she came over to look at the rock, too.

"It's not some prank," Wade protested grimly as he handed the rock to his mother. "It was deliberate destruction of property. Someone should speak to the boys' parents, whoever they are."

His mother gasped and then let the rock fall back to the floor. She shook her head. "I don't know if we should involve the parents. Sometimes they don't know what to do for boys that have trouble."

Wade wasn't sure what was making his mother so nervous, but he figured it could only be one thing. "You were a good parent to me—and to my brothers, too. I'm sure we never told you that often enough, but you always seemed to know what we needed. You did the best you could."

"Did I?" his mother asked, uncertainty in her voice. "I sat in my cell for years, wondering what I should have done for you boys."

"You did fine," Wade said, his voice gruff. The wind had picked up outside, and a flurry of fine snow came in through the broken window. The old house rattled slightly.

But his mother was looking at him like he should say something else, so he added, "I'm sure Jake and Tyler feel the same way I do."

"Your brothers were a little easier than you," his mother admitted as she stepped closer and put her hand out to touch his cheek. Her palm was warm against his jaw. "But then, you were the oldest. The one who wanted to protect us all. The one I failed the most."

She took her hand away and let it fall to her side.

"No." Wade shook his head. "You didn't—"

There was a shy knock, and Wade looked behind his mother to see Amy standing in the doorway. She had a gray wool scarf wound around her head, and her lips were pale, as though she were still cold. She had clearly walked over like she'd planned and she had a white pillowcase in her hands filled with something lumpy.

His mother was still facing his direction though. She was looking down at the floor, and Wade sensed she had something she needed to say, so he didn't mention that anyone else was here.

Amy let the pillowcase rest on the floor, and she stood motionless, her gloved hands pressed together in what might be prayer or maybe just nerves.

Finally, his mother spoke. "I was the one who didn't listen to you. That morning before all this happened. I'm sorry I didn't listen. Will you ever forgive me?"

"What—?" Wade asked. "What do you mean?"

"I learned in prison that truth is very important. It cleanses something inside of us," his mother continued, struggling with the words.

"You don't need to—" Wade had heard her confession only once before, when she was before the judge. That was sufficient for him.

He risked a glance over at Amy and saw

the pain of the situation reflected in her face, as well. Her eyes were black wells of pity, and she was looking straight at him. He wanted to go to her and shield her in his arms, but he couldn't move.

"It's not for me," his mother said softly as she finally raised her eyes to him.

He knew something awful was coming, but he couldn't imagine what it was. His family had been torn apart in the worst way possible. He didn't think they had any secrets left. Amy murmured a protest, but his mother was too intense to notice any distractions.

"Did my father do something even worse?" That was the only thing Wade could imagine that there would be left to tell in his family.

His mother shook her head. "Don't make me say the words. I know it was my fault for not listening to you. That's why I took the blame. That morning right here in this kitchen—you told me you wished he was dead—that you couldn't stand to live with him any longer. I was your mother. I should have seen you were at your breaking point. I should never have put you in a position where you felt you had to do what you did."

Wade felt a ringing in his ears. He couldn't be hearing right. Instinctively, he looked over at Amy, and she took a step toward him, coming into the kitchen and standing there, her eyes even darker than before. And her face was so white. He could see the exact instant she realized what his mother was implying. Her eyes filled with horror, and she stepped back, as though she'd seen something awful. It's the only thing that helped him see it, too.

"You think I killed him," Wade said, the words coming out so thin and disjointed that he didn't recognize his own voice. "You think I killed my father."

He heard a whimper of pain from Amy's lips, but he couldn't bear to look at her. He knew the revulsion he would see. Nothing as horrible as murder should ever touch Amy's life. He'd thought that when his father was killed, and he thought it again today. The only difference was that, now, he couldn't keep it away from her by leaving town. She would always remember him as a murderer.

The other meaning of his mother's words finally came to him. He stared at her. "You didn't do it? Kill him?"

She shook her head and then bowed it in what looked like defeat. "I couldn't let them punish you. It was my fault as much as yours. I knew you boys suffered. Until you said what you did that day, I just never imagined it was so bad that you would—"

"Oh," Amy said then, sounding as though all of the air had gone out of her lungs.

Wade had no choice but to look at her, to plead with her. "I didn't do it. I may have been angry and said I wanted him dead, but that's all. It wasn't me."

There was absolute silence for a moment, and Wade thought he would very much like to preserve that moment of time. It was like the summer night as a boy when he'd ridden a rusty old Ferris wheel that was parked along the highway. On one round, it had stopped, letting him swing high over the world below. Until the wheel started moving again, he didn't need to worry about what was coming next or what had gone before. He was high up and alone in the world.

It was Amy who broke the silence. She gave a cry of anguish and turned to leave.

"Please," Wade begged as he took a step toward her.

She turned to him, and the look in her eyes stopped him from going to her.

"I knew you weren't coming back, but I never imagined it was because—" She stopped like she couldn't go on, then she whispered, "How could you?"

Wade knew then that some part of him had always counted on Amy—even when he hadn't seen her for all of those years—some part of her made his world bearable. He had his memories of her, and they warmed his heart. She had believed in him all those years while they grew up. As she turned to run away, he knew he had lost the most precious thing in his life. She would no longer think of him with fondness. Not even when she remembered their past together. She was lost to him forever, in the most final way. She despised him.

He didn't quite realize his cheeks were damp until his mother touched his arm. Even then, he couldn't believe he was crying. He hadn't shed a tear when he took that tumble in the last rodeo and had broken more bones than he'd known a man possessed. The doctor had given him something to bite down on for the pain, but there hadn't been a need for any tissue for tears.

"I'm sorry. I didn't know anyone was here," his mother said hoarsely.

Wade blinked back his last tear. "It's not your fault. Nothing is your fault."

Then he opened his arms and embraced his mother like he hadn't been able to do when he came home last night. For the first time, he realized all she had given up by accepting the label of murderer. And she had done it for him.

"I never would have said anything to Amy," his mother whispered. "I know what she means to you."

"Hush, it's okay," he said as he stood there and rocked her in his arms.

The only thing he could think was that they never should have gone into Dry Creek this morning. They were not ready to face their past; it was no wonder if the people here were not ready to face it, either.

He heard the sound of a door banging and looked up only to realize the wind had blown open the screen door to the porch. No one was there. Amy hadn't come back. And he refused to go to the window to see if she had made it back to her home yet. He needed to let her go.

Amy stood in the cold, leaning on the side of her house, breathing deeply and letting the tears flow down her face. She couldn't seem to stop them. She'd been so proud of herself for making her own choice in the matter when she walked over to the Stone ranch fifteen minutes ago. But now she only felt wounded. And betrayed. Had Wade really killed his father? He said he hadn't, but Gracie apparently hadn't done it, either, and someone had to have lifted that shovel.

She heard the door of the house open, but she didn't see it. She was around the corner.

"Amy?" Her aunt's voice came to her on the wind, sounding querulous. "Where are you? Shawn's on the telephone for you. I saw you come running across the fields."

Amy could barely breathe. She couldn't

talk. So she kept leaning against the side of the house, hidden from her aunt, seeking any warmth she could find in the wood that had sheltered her family since before she was born.

She stayed there for a long time, letting the chill seep into her body, deeper and deeper. She remembered her fear this morning that people would pity her for not having the courage to do something with her life. Now, that seemed the slightest of things to worry about. What became of women who loved murderers anyway? Did they shrink from the men they cared about more and more over time? Did they ever grow accustomed to it?

She told herself that she didn't know if Wade had murdered his father. He said he hadn't, and he could be telling the truth. But she would never be sure one way or the other. She didn't even know how she could be close to him without having that question answered. She had loved him for years and still did, but that wasn't enough. She needed to trust him, too.

Amy stayed standing there until she saw the white flecks on her wool scarf. It was snowing more. Only then did something break inside her so she could pray. She knelt down and bowed her head. No words came to her, but she poured her grief and confusion out to God, anyway. She felt like He was listening, but maybe it was just her exhaustion calming her and not really His presence. She didn't know what—or who—to trust anymore.

A few minutes later, she heard the door to the house open again. She heard hesitant footsteps until, finally, she saw Aunt Tilly come around the corner. She had her father's coat draped over her robe, and an old cap on her head.

"What's wrong?" her aunt asked in a voice Amy hadn't heard much of lately. Her aunt was worried about her.

"It's that Stone boy, isn't it?" her aunt said gently as she gathered Amy up and

CROSS CANCER
INSTITUTE - GIFT SHOP
11560 University Avenue
Edmonton AB

10/20/2022 2:34:27 PM   Tomiko

$1.00 Books $1.00 Tx1

SUB TOTAL $1.00
GST $0.05

TOTAL   **$1.05**
Cash $1.05
Item count: 1
Trans:30781   Terminal:050014012-100001

All Items are FINAL SALE!

GST#R124072513

THANK YOU & COME BACK

into her arms. "No one ever said the Stone men weren't charming enough to break a woman's heart. It was true then—it's true now."

Amy let herself be led inside. She had dried grass and twigs on her jeans from where she had knelt and mud on her shoes from where she had stood, but her aunt didn't say anything about the dirt as she led Amy into the kitchen.

"I'm going to fix you a nice cup of cocoa," her aunt said as she sat Amy down in a chair at the table. "You'll feel better in no time at all."

Amy knew that wasn't true, but she didn't correct her. She needed her family now more than ever.

It wasn't until she was getting ready for bed that night that Amy realized she had left her sack in the enclosed porch of the Stone place. Inside were her favorite Christmas ornaments, the ones that had belonged to her parents. They weren't expensive, but they were some of the few things she had from them. She only used the ornaments to decorate her bedroom, so she knew her aunt wouldn't miss them.

In her earlier enthusiasm, Amy had wanted to share the ornaments with Gracie to show how happy she was that the other woman had come home.

Amy crawled under the covers and turned out her bedside light. She'd have to ask Gracie for the sack back, of course. She doubted the other woman would want any ornaments around her. Not this year, not when she would have to worry about who had murdered Buck Stone. For the first time, it occurred to her that Wade might go to prison if he was guilty.

She didn't sleep that night, but she did lie in bed and stare into the darkness, trying to summon up the words to pray. This morning she had worried her life was boring, and now it felt like a nightmare. Should she tell anyone about the conversation she had overheard? Was she legally obligated to do so? Gracie wouldn't tell anyone else of her suspicions about Wade—at least, Amy didn't think so. Not if she loved her son enough to go to prison in his place.

It was almost dawn when Amy remembered it was Sunday. Charley Nelson was going to drive out and get her since the pickup wasn't working. Her grandfather had an old Jeep he sometimes drove places, but he didn't let anyone else use it.

And Charley insisted on giving her a ride. He had already invited her to dinner after church so they could talk about the Christmas sleigh. Some of the painted elves on the sleigh needed a touch-up, and she'd offered to do it for Charley, since the arthritis in his hands was troubling him this year. Maybe somewhere in the discussion of paint and elf hats, she could find a way to ask him what she should do.

"Oh, Lord, give me wisdom," she whispered.

Feeling more at peace, her eyes drifted closed. An hour later her alarm rang.

She woke with the thought that no one in the world knew more about the painful side of love than God did. He knew what she should do. In the comfort of that realization, she swung her legs out of bed. She needed to face the day.

Chapter Four

Wade sat in the back pew of the Dry Creek church and ran his finger around the collar of the white dress shirt his mother had insisted he wear. She'd found it this morning in the back closet of her old bedroom, still wrapped in its original plastic along with a thin, black tie. He knew his father had never worn either the shirt or the tie, and that's what made Wade willing to put them on.

All his life, Wade had refused to wear white shirts, thinking they made him look like a waiter or, even worse, some guy in a casket. As for ties, the less said the better. And yet here he was. Trussed up like a Christmas turkey and trying to get used to it.

He glanced down to be sure there wasn't any dirt on his boots before looking straight ahead.

Pastor Curtis had already started the sermon when Wade and his mother had slipped into church. The man wore glasses now and had aged since Wade had last seen him. But he hadn't missed a beat when he saw the two of them. He recognized them with a smile and a brief nod in their direction, but his voice hadn't wavered, and nothing about him screamed that he'd just seen two criminals sneak into the church when no one else was watching.

Wade was grateful to him.

He tried to keep his mind busy by looking around. He figured there had to be eighty people in this place, half of them on the same side of the church as he and his mother. He should recognize them, but all he could see were the backs of their heads, and everyone's hair style had no doubt changed since he'd known them, so he didn't even try to guess who they were.

After he counted heads, he let his gaze wander.

Sunlight was pouring into the church through the row of windows on each side, and it showed up every smudge on the walls and several purple stains on the carpet. Wade smiled a little. He guessed children were not only allowed in this church but given some freedom, too. It looked like Kool-Aid had spilled at some point, and some of the marks on the walls matched little fingers.

He'd only been inside the church a couple of times as a boy, but he did know that the paint had been changed to yellow, replacing beige, and the pew cushions that used to be brown were now a dark gray. On the wall behind the pulpit, a pine wreath was hanging that had cones and bright red berries all over it. The berries were probably fake ones, but the smell of the pine meant the needles were definitely real. It was obvious the people in this church loved Christmas and weren't afraid to show it.

He paused. Then he said the word Christmas again to himself.

The muscles in his neck didn't tighten up at the mention of the day like they used to. For the past nine years, when he thought of the holiday, he'd teetered on the edge of a horrible guilt. But he had pieced it together last night. If his mother hadn't killed his father, then Wade's argument with his father hadn't pushed her to do it. So he hadn't played any part in the murder.

He was a free man—except for sitting here in the church, of course. Wade must have fidgeted some at the thought, because his mother put her hand on his arm. To please her, he tried to be still and focus.

He had only been listening for a few minutes when the pastor said something about a man named Lazarus and how Jesus had raised him from the dead, just like He can raise everyone from their death of sin. Wade paused for a moment to wonder how many in the church believed what the pastor was saying. It would sure make his mother's homecoming easier if even half of them did. He wasn't a big advocate of sin, but he figured the knowledge that a person was guilty would keep him humble when it came to judging others.

Wade could only listen for a little while, and then his eyes strayed to the other side of the church where Amy sat. It wasn't the first time he'd looked over at her this morning. He liked the way her blond hair was wrapped up in a fancy twist until it looked like a crown. The sunshine on her hair was enough to make her glow. But then she also had on gold earrings that dangled down and moved every time she did anything. She literally sparkled. He wondered briefly if the angels in heaven would look like her as they sat up there polishing their wings.

He told himself he couldn't sit and stare at Amy for the whole hour. He was only tormenting himself by even glancing over at her. She had not turned around once so she didn't even know he and his mother were in the church. He had no idea if she would greet them if she knew.

He had spent half of the night wondering if Amy believed he'd actually committed a murder—of anyone, let alone his father. He'd spent the other half wondering who had done it since neither he nor his mother had. No one had ever suggested it had been a stranger. For one thing, his father wouldn't have been sitting there, seemingly relaxed, on a bale of hay if a salesman or lost traveler had come in off the road. He would have been standing up and yelling at them that they were trespassing and they better get off his place right now, or else.

Wade hadn't asked the question aloud yet, but it was burning inside him. Had the murderer been one of his brothers? He hurt to think so, but anyone else would have needed to drive a vehicle onto the property, and his mother would have heard it. Surely if she had heard an engine, she wouldn't have assumed Wade had been the one to lift that shovel. No, it had to be someone close.

Just then, the pastor said everyone should stand up so they could sing the final hymn. There was a fair amount of rustling as people stood up, straightened their clothes, took a hymnal from the rack in front of them and, in the case of one woman, twisted around to lay a sleeping toddler back down on the pew.

Wade held his breath when he saw the woman turn. He didn't remember her name, but she was Mrs. Hargrove's daughter. Blond hair, pleasant face and somewhere in her forties. Nice woman. Doris June, that was her name.

The last he'd seen her, Doris June had been working in Anchorage and he had pestered her with questions about polar bears. She'd been almost twenty years older than him so he only knew her from when she had come back to visit her mother. He continued to watch her as she straightened up after laying down the child. She was facing the back of the church, so she was looking right at him. Wade knew the minute she recognized him and his mother.

"Mrs. Stone!" Doris June exclaimed, surprise flooding her face. She did nothing to quiet her voice. "And Wade! You're back!"

Wade didn't hear any horror in the woman's voice, but she couldn't have made a more dramatic announcement than if she had said a flock of pigeons had just landed in the back pew. In all corners of the church, every sound stopped. Forgetting about that final hymn the pastor wanted, the woman playing the piano turned to stare at Wade and his mother.

It was completely silent, and Wade stood in place.

Finally, a child somewhere, probably sensing the tension in the place, started to cry. No one even bent to comfort the poor babe.

Wade reached up and loosened the knot on his tie. He was tempted to take the thing off altogether, but too many eyes were watching him. He should have known his mother's efforts to make them respectable were going to fail.

His eyes glanced down at the top of her head. His mother was facing the crowd with bravery, and that was all he could do, too. He shifted his body, making his stance more aggressive than it had been. And he let his eyes roam over the people, meeting each gaze until the other person glanced away, whether in fear or shame, he didn't much care.

And then his eyes met Amy's. The anguish she felt was clear on her face. She gazed steadily into his eyes, but he could tell tears were starting to form. He knew, not because he could see them, but simply because he'd seen her face in every possible emotion. He knew her so well it physically hurt him to see her in distress. He was the first to look away.

Pastor Curtis finally cleared his throat. "The final hymn is 'He Leadeth Me.' Page two hundred and fifty-six. We'll sing the first and last verses only."

One by one, people turned around until they faced the pulpit again. The pianist started to play the hymn. By the time the pastor started to sing, people had regained enough of their senses to join in. Wade felt relief go through him as he listened to the voices raised in unison.

Midway through the first few sentences of the song, his mother nudged him. She held an open hymnal out to him. He nodded and started holding a corner of the book, but he didn't sing. He couldn't. The words of the song penetrated his mind and left him breathless with yearning. He wished someone could lead him where he needed to go. If ever he needed help, it was now

When he'd left Dry Creek nine years ago, he'd thought that the worst of his life was over—that nothing could be as devastating as hearing his mother confess that she had killed his father. But he'd been wrong.

This was worse. He didn't understand anything now.

The music stopped, and the pastor asked everyone to bow their heads for prayer. For the first time in his life, Wade did so. He didn't know much about prayer, and he figured God wouldn't listen to him anyway. But in this church, he wasn't praying alone. Surely, God would listen to the prayers of these people.

"…and help us to be accepting of our neighbors, filled with love and kindness for each other," Pastor Curtis finished. "In our Lord's name, Amen."

The words eased some of Wade's pain and he opened his eyes with hope.

He was struck anew with how ordinary the people here were. There were no designer clothes among them. Not many clothes that even looked new. Most faces had a wrinkle or two, and everyone wore sensible shoes and carried heavy coats. He doubted there was more than twenty dollars in anyone's pocket.

But these were good people. He was beginning to think that they would accept their old neighbors back. So, he gave a nod to a few of them, and they cautiously nodded at him, too.

He and his mother did not have time to leave their pew before Mrs. Hargrove came rushing over to them. Wade hadn't seen her since he left here, but she hadn't changed much. He thought he still recognized the red, gingham dress she wore, although the gold pin gathering up the neckline was new. Her hair was grayer, but it was held back with the same kind of amber-colored plastic clip she used to wear. Her face had always been angular and weathered, but there was nothing slowing down her smile.

As soon as she got close enough, she reached out to take his mother's hand.

"Gracie Stone." Mrs. Hargrove said the name with love, and Wade could have kissed her for it. "I just knew you were going to show up here before long," the older woman continued, her eyes shining. "My last letter was returned yesterday. Oh—" She looked at his mother for a full moment longer as her smile stretched even bigger. "It's so good to see you. Welcome home."

In return, his mother did the most amazing thing. She held her arms out and hugged the older woman like she wasn't planning to ever let her go.

Wade had never known his mother to hug anyone. He used to think it had something to do with her Cherokee heritage. But she'd changed in prison. She had embraced him several times yesterday as they worried about what to do next. And now, here she was with her arms wrapped around Mrs. Hargrove, someone she hadn't seen in almost a decade.

Maybe his mother had learned something about God while she was gone, after all. She'd certainly learned about sharing her emotions.

When she finally drew away from the other woman, his mother's eyes were damp. "I never did congratulate you properly on your marriage, Mrs. Hargrove. Or is it Mrs. Nelson now?"

The older woman grinned. "I answer to both. I've been Mrs. Hargrove my whole life and Charley doesn't mind if folks keep on calling me that. It's a hard habit for them to break after all these years. Besides, Charley knows he's got his rightful place in my heart. He's not going to fret about a name."

"Charley Nelson?" Wade asked, putting the pieces together. The two older people had been friends ever since their spouses died many years ago. He didn't have a chance to add his congratulations before Charley came up to him with his hand stretched out.

"My arthritis is slowing me down a little so Edith beat me over here." The man shook Wade's hand and then glanced at his wife with deep affection in his eyes before turning back to Wade. "But I'm going to beat her to the punch by asking if you'd both like to come eat with us. Edith has a pot roast in the oven and we'd be tickled to sit and visit with you."

"I don't know—" Wade tried to think of an excuse. He thought it would be safer if he and his mother left, before people recovered from the surprise that they were even here. But he was hungry, and they'd used the last of the eggs this morning for an early breakfast. All they had left at the ranch were those cans of soup.

"We're meeting to talk about the Christmas sleigh," Charley added and then looked at Wade with a grin. "I remember how you used to like that sleigh."

"Yes, but—"

"Well, I'm looking for someone to drive it this year. It's too much for me to handle with my hands being all crippled up like they have been." Charley held out his hands.

Wade could see the swollen knuckles and gnarled fingers.

"They're a working man's hands, all right," Wade said gently. "You should be proud of them."

He noticed Mrs. Hargrove and his mother had stopped talking so they could listen.

Charley nodded. "You'd be doing an old man a real service if you'd help out this year."

Wade took a deep breath, figuring he would have to use some fancy words to decline this one. Especially because he recognized the kindness behind the request.

"He's always wanted to drive that sleigh," his mother said before Wade could speak. "I always felt bad that Buck never let the sleigh come to our place. But Wade would love to drive it."

"I figured as much," Charley said in satisfaction. "I remember he used to sit and stare at the thing when we were getting ready for the Christmas Eve run. For most kids, it was just the presents, but Wade sure liked the sleigh, too. It's settled then."

Wade wasn't quite sure how it had been decided without his agreement, but the older people were all looking so pleased that he didn't have the heart to say he wouldn't do it. He had a bad feeling about what could happen, though—not everyone was as openhearted as Charley and his wife.

But maybe he was making too much of everything. Besides, if he had a winter coat on and a scarf wrapped around his face, people might not even know who was driving the sleigh around in the dark. People tended to pay more attention to the horses than the driver, anyway; at least, that's how he remembered it. He was about to ask Charley if he still had the same pair of chestnut mares, when Mrs. Hargrove spoke.

"Oh, and Amy is coming to dinner, too," she said as she gathered a worn, black purse closer to her side and looked up at Wade. "It'll be a great time for you both to get reacquainted. So much time has passed, but I remember how the two of you used to sit and talk."

"I don't think—" he began.

But the older couple was already walking down the aisle with his mother between them.

He shook his head in dismay.

That's when he saw Amy. She was wearing a deep blue sweater that made her eyes change and shimmer like moonlight on a dark winter night when the stars seemed most distant. And she had a golden heart hanging from a thin chain around her neck. She was pure good- ness, and he felt sad at the hesitation in her eyes. He didn't know how long she'd been listening or if she had heard what Mrs. Hargrove had said about them.

He wondered who had given Amy the heart necklace, but he couldn't dare ask. He did know she hadn't been wearing it yesterday when he checked for hidden rings on chains around her neck, so it must not be that important to her. At least, he hoped not.

He blinked a few times, not knowing what to say, and she was still standing there, looking at him. There was only one thing to do—confess.

"Charley invited me for dinner after church," he finally said, his face flushed like he'd done something wrong. "And my mother, of course. But I can refuse. I can always come back and get my mother after she's done."

He felt like he needed to straighten his tie again, but if he did, he was afraid he wouldn't be able to swallow.

"I could say I'm not feeling well," he stammered. "And that'd be halfway to the truth. Or I could go to the café. Yes, the café. I'll have a nice hamburger. And some fries."

They were both silent for a moment, looking at each other without any of the usual warmth of friends. Wade noticed for the first time that she had a light freckle on her right cheekbone. The sunlight brought it out. He wondered if she even knew it was there, and if she did, did she worry about it? At least, there was no bandage covering it up.

"The café isn't open on Sunday," Amy finally said, turning her face away from him. "I don't think the places in Miles City are open, either."

"Ah, well, we have a can of beef broth

out at the ranch," Wade assured her. "I think I could find some crackers, too. And if my mother stays in town to eat, I'll be fine."

It wouldn't be the first meal he'd missed in his life, he told himself, just before his stomach growled.

Amy looked at him for another minute and then sighed. "No one passes up Mrs. Hargrove's pot roast. She uses root vegetables stored from her garden. Onions. Carrots. Those little red potatoes. You won't find anything better anywhere."

His stomach unclenched when Amy gave him a hint of a smile.

"And she'll probably have pie for dessert," she added as she lifted her eyebrow in what seemed like a gesture of defeat.

He wondered if she was remembering how much he enjoyed the pie she had made for him when she was thirteen.

"Either lemon or blueberry," she added. "Those are Charley's favorites."

"No apple?" he asked. That had been

the kind Amy had made for him. They'd taken it, along with two forks, down to the coulee one early autumn day and had enjoyed a feast. The sun had been shining, and she'd had a speck of cinnamon sugar on her cheek. It was the first time Wade had ever thought about kissing her. He'd been fifteen and it had taken him two years to work up the nerve to really do it, but from the time of the pie, he must have thought about it every single day until then.

Something flickered through Amy's eyes. She remembered that day but wasn't going to own up to it.

She did shake her head. "No apple."

"Well, regardless of what kind of pie it is, I'll like it," he said, trying to read her face. "I guess I should go then—to dinner."

She nodded at him and turned to walk down the aisle. He couldn't do anything but follow her. And then he couldn't help but notice the gentle sway of the full-length winter coat she wore. And the way her red, knit scarf was twisted around her neck in some kind of a fashion knot. Who was she dressing up to see in church, anyway?

Wade looked behind him with a scowl and saw Shawn. The man's hair still had that indistinct color that was neither blond nor brown, but he'd filled out some since Wade had seen him, and there was nothing undecided about the fierce expression on his plain, broad face. He was protecting what was his, and he didn't want Wade around.

So, that's the way it was, Wade thought to himself. Amy might say the man was only interested in her for the sake of his political ambitions, but she was wrong. The poor guy was even wearing a black business suit, with creases in the pants' legs that came from an honest-to-goodness iron, and a tie knotted so close under his neck he could hardly swallow. Wade figured there was little doubt that his old classmate was in love, especially if he was the one who had used that iron.

Sunlight filtered into Mrs. Hargrove's dining room even though the night's frost was still melting on the window panes. Wallpaper with pink cabbage roses covered the upper part of the room and white wood trim outlined the doorways. The sounds of Charley moving the chairs around mingled with the noise of the oven opening and closing. The smell of roasting beef came floating in from the kitchen and would be pleasant on any other day. Amy willed herself to relax. She'd had Sunday dinner in this room many times.

But never, she was forced to admit, like this. Usually Mrs. Hargrove used her green stoneware plates and plain water glasses. Amy looked down at the linen napkin, folded into the shape of a swan and now resting on the gold-rimmed china plate in front of her. Mrs. Hargrove was using her wedding dishes, the ones she'd been given forty-some years ago when she'd married her first husband. Amy had taken a peek at the back of one plate and noted they were made by Lenox. And Gracie had offered to fold the napkins, saying she'd learned how to do several patterns when she'd been in prison.

Amy expected the remark about prison would lead Gracie to make a bold declaration of her innocence—even if she didn't say she thought Wade was guilty. But the other woman didn't say anything more about it.

From some place in her china cabinet, Mrs. Hargrove had earlier found crystal goblets, and now Charley was setting one by each of the five plates. The rectangular table had been pushed into a corner and Amy had been squeezed onto a short bench she had never even seen before. She didn't know where Charley had put the chairs that were usually on this side of the table and she was reluctant to ask.

The older man had looked very satisfied with himself as he had rushed her and Wade onto this bench almost before they had even taken their coats off. He insisted they needed time alone to get to know each other again, and so they should sit and visit while he helped Edith and Gracie get everything ready.

Amy knew she shouldn't have trusted a man her grandfather's age, who was being so helpful about getting the table ready for Sunday dinner.

Both she and Wade had protested that they could help, too, but Charley got a reproachful look on his face. So they sat there—like two stone lions squashed together in some ancient ruin that had fallen on hard times—until Charley went into the kitchen saying he was going to see if his wife needed help carving the roast.

Being alone with Wade gave Amy a jittery feeling. She told herself it was because he might be a murderer, but she thought it was just him. She twirled the swan napkin around on her plate and then remembered her purse was on her lap. She opened it and took out a packet of gum.

"Care for some?" Politeness demanded she hold the packet of spearmint out to Wade.

He smiled, and said he'd rather watch her chew it.

"A little gum won't hurt you," she said, feeling defensive even as she said the words. She knew the gum was a nervous habit, and that it was probably destroying her teeth.

"I'm not so sure it's harmless," Wade said as he watched her slip the stick of gum into her mouth. And then he grinned, looking like he was seventeen again. "But we can't always take the safe road through life, now can we?"

There didn't seem to be anything to say to that, so she just sat there. No one was taking any road as far as she was concerned. At least not the two of them. And definitely not together. She thought he might have slid a little closer while she was opening her purse. She couldn't be sure, but she tried to slide closer to the wall to make up for it, just in case.

"The house has been here over fifty years," Wade said. "Those walls aren't going to budge."

She didn't know how he knew she'd tried to move since he had been looking straight ahead. Then she wondered if she would take up less room if she held her breath. That would be hard to do when she was chewing gum, though.

Finally, she decided to just ignore him, and it was blissfully silent for a couple of minutes.

Then Mrs. Hargrove walked out of the kitchen, holding a platter piled high with slices of pot roast and vegetables. Gracie followed with a basket of the golden-brown biscuits that were Mrs. Hargrove's specialty. Charley came last with a butter dish in one hand and what looked like a jar of his wife's chokecherry jam in the other.

"I wouldn't mind sitting closer to the kitchen," Amy offered, trying to sound casual. "That way, I can get up and get anything you might need. Salt. Pepper. That kind of thing."

"Aren't you sweet to offer?" Mrs. Hargrove said as she put the platter on the table and sat down in her own chair, which happened to one of the wood ones with solid arms and plenty of room for sitting that were usually at the table. Apparently, Charley hadn't hidden the chairs he, his wife and Gracie were going to be using.

Amy was going to add something to what she'd said, but Mrs. Hargrove reached over and moved the basket of biscuits that Gracie had placed on the table. They were now closer to Wade.

"You're fine right where you're sitting

now, dear," she said in response to Amy's unspoken question. "Besides, I know where everything is, so I can get it easy enough."

By then, Gracie and Charley had found their places at the table, as well.

"It's just—" Amy began again.

"You're comfortable there, aren't you dear?" Mrs. Hargrove turned and gave her a partial smile. It was the same tilting of her lips that she had used when she'd been Amy's Sunday school teacher and taught her and the other children how to—what did she call it? Oh, yes, "persevere in adversity." It's what the apostles had done and what Mrs. Hargrove expected them to do, even though the only adversity they had known in their young lives were the squabbles they had with each other.

"I'm fine," Amy said. No one let Mrs. Hargrove down.

Amy told herself she was probably making too much of it, anyway. She didn't really mind being pressed against the wall. It was a good, solid surface. Although it did make her feel like a wildflower being pressed between the pages of a heavy reference book. But she wasn't that delicate, and there was no real harm done. No, it wasn't the wall that bothered her at all.

It was the force on the other side of her who made her nervous.

Wade.

She'd never really appreciated just how solid he was until she was squeezed against him. She could hardly ignore the bulging muscles of his arm against hers, but she couldn't say anything, either. It would not be polite dinner conversation. And, it wasn't just his arm. It was all of him. He was somehow larger sitting down than he had been standing. She certainly didn't remember him being like this when they were kids.

In all the meals she'd had at Mrs. Hargrove's house, Amy had never seen two guests seated so close together. Wade had shaved this morning, and when she'd first sat down, she had caught whiffs of after-shave whenever he moved. She thought she'd been able to smell the soap he used, too, until Mrs. Hargrove had brought in the platter of pot roast.

"Remember, I have some dinner set aside in the kitchen for your aunt and grandfather," Mrs. Hargrove said, look-ing at Amy. "Plenty of pot roast and a few biscuits to go with it."

"They'll appreciate it," Amy said.

Mrs. Hargrove nodded as though glad that was settled and inclined her head toward her husband.

"Let's pray." Charley bowed his head.

Everyone else followed. Amy remem-bered her gum and quickly removed it.

"Lord, You have blessed us greatly," Charley said, his voice slow and rich. "This is a fine-looking meal. And we're grateful we can share it with our friends here. Help them to each find a new start in life with Your help. In Jesus' name. Amen."

When Amy opened her eyes, she saw Mrs. Hargrove look at her husband in exasperation.

"You didn't even mention the missionaries. Or the people on the prayer chain," the older woman scolded. "Or the preparations for the nativity pageant. The angels need more practice, you know."

Amy felt Wade's arm brush against her as he lifted his crystal goblet filled with ice water.

Charley shook his head. "I'll get to all of them when we say grace tonight. Right now, I'm hungry, and everything smells too good. Besides, I prayed for new starts in life, and we want to eat so we old folks can sit in the kitchen and give those two young lovebirds a chance to get working on that start."

Amy gasped, and Wade's drink of water evidently went down the wrong way, because he started coughing.

"Need a thump on the back?" Charley asked as he pushed back his chair and then stood. "You'll have to turn to your left so I can get in a good whack."

"I don't think—" Wade started to sputter, but then he started to cough again.

"A good thump is all that'll cure you, son," Charley said as he took another step closer to Wade and bent down. "Just give a half turn to your left."

Amy looked to her right as Wade turned to his left and almost started to cough herself. Or cry. They were face-to-face and much too close. Seeing him made her freeze. Charley might think they were lovebirds, but Wade reminded her as more of a hawk. A very predatory one who had already sighted his prey.

She looked away again. With that expression on his face, he looked like he could be a criminal. Maybe not a murderer, but certainly one of those men who stole every dime from some poor widow woman.

Fortunately, once she looked away, she couldn't see Wade. But she could hear him. His breathing was steady again. Apparently the shock of seeing her so close had made the cough disappear. Charley didn't need to thump him on the back after all.

The older man sat down in his chair and Amy squirmed.

"Sorry," Wade said, and she turned to look at him.

"I need to get out," she said, trying to be quiet about it. His breathing might be smooth, but hers was not. Maybe if she had a moment in the kitchen to collect her feelings, she would be able to sit here without wanting to bite her fingernails down to the quick.

Wade wordlessly slid over to the end of the bench and then stood up. "Maybe it would be better if I just stood here until dinner's over."

"You can't eat pot roast standing up," Charley protested as he put his napkin back on his plate. "You just hang on, and I'll go get each of you one of those chairs."

Looking guilty, Charley glanced at his wife as he stood up.

"I told you it wouldn't work," she chided him mildly. "You can't make people get close to each other just because you sit them that way."

"Well, it worked for us." Charley started walking toward the living room. "That and your pie, of course."

Mrs. Hargrove shook her head as her husband left the room. Then she turned to Amy. "I'm sorry. My husband is a bit too romantic for his own good."

Amy knew the older woman meant well, but they couldn't change course now. Amy finished sliding off the bench. "I'll be back."

She moved by Wade and didn't even look at him.

"Are you all right?" Mrs. Hargrove asked her as she walked by. "Your face looks a little flushed. Maybe you have a fever."

"Maybe so," Amy said.

Then she fled to the kitchen.

Please, Lord, she thought. *Let me have a fever. That would be a much better excuse than that I was concerned about Wade's arm. I can't go back in there after this.*

And then she realized in dismay, *I don't even have my car with me, Lord. I have to go back in there.*

She hadn't done something so foolish in a long time.

Chapter Five

❧

Wade felt like the air had gone out of the room. Everything smelled the same and looked the same, but it was all different. He stood there staring across the space to the kitchen door, which had closed behind Amy, almost as though he might find some pattern in its oak grain that would explain the hollow feeling growing inside him.

It was his fault, of course. He should have declined the dinner invitation, no matter what Amy had said.

Finally, he looked down at his mother and Mrs. Hargrove. The two women were seated at the table, their pink linen napkins in their laps, and almost identical expressions of sympathy on their dear faces.

"I'm afraid it's me," he whispered.

He didn't bother to disguise the bleakness in his voice. He shouldn't have let his guard down. Sitting there with Amy, smelling that spearmint gum, had felt so right to him that he'd forgotten everything had changed between them. She couldn't bear to even sit beside him.

"Oh, no, I'm sure it's not you," Mrs. Hargrove said. The bracing tone of her voice told him as nothing else could that his situation with Amy was hopeless. "It's just that bench. Charley should never have brought the thing to the dinner table."

His mother was quick to nod her agreement. "That must be it. We used to have a bench like that in our group sessions in prison. Yours is much nicer, of course." She glanced apologetically at her friend. "I'm sure you would never have a prison bench in your house. I just meant that some people felt squeezed when they sat on the thing, as if they needed more room. It had nothing to do with who they were or who was seated next to them—well, usually not, at least."

His mother flushed suddenly, obviously remembering something she'd forgotten.

Wade suspected the prison bench did more than make people uncomfortable. And that, as often as not, it did have something to do with the person seated beside them. It was unlikely that bench had been responsible for breaking any-one's heart, though. At least, not like his was broken.

The bay window in the room made a slight creaking sound and Wade glanced over at it, grateful for the distraction. A bare tree swayed in the yard from the force of the wind. The sun had gone behind some storm clouds, and the day had turned heavy and gray.

"That wind's coming from the north," he muttered, half to himself.

"It'll snow then. And turn colder," his mother said, turning to look at him. "Although I don't suppose it matters very much."

They were silent for a moment.

"Maybe you better excuse me, too," he finally said. One thing did matter very much. "I want to see that Amy is all right."

"You do that," Mrs. Hargrove said with a nod, the relief evident in her voice. "She's usually a very calm girl. Nothing bothers her. Of course, she keeps everything inside."

Wade glanced at his mother. She was sitting too still, her face expressionless.

"I expect Amy has her reasons if she's upset," Wade said.

"I'm sure she does," his mother agreed, but didn't say anything more.

Wade felt a sudden urge to unburden himself and tell Mrs. Hargrove what had happened, but he couldn't seem to gather up the words.

"Well, I'll be back," he said instead and began to walk toward the kitchen.

"Tell her I have a chair for her," Charley called out as he came in from the living room.

Wade turned to look at the man and then nodded. "I'm sure she'd like that."

Charley had brought back two wooden chairs, exactly like the ones everyone else had. Good, solid chairs. A person sitting in one of them wouldn't need to worry about touching another living being if she didn't want to.

One doorway was all that separated the dining room from the kitchen, but Wade felt like he walked a mile to get there. He didn't know what to say to Amy except that he was leaving. He didn't want her to miss dinner just because she couldn't sit beside him. He'd wait out in his pickup until his mother was through eating.

The first thing Wade saw when he

walked into Mrs. Hargrove's kitchen was Amy standing there with her eyes closed and her hand on her forehead as though she was getting ready to faint, like in some old melodrama. He forgot all about what he was going to say. He took several quick steps to her side and reached out to catch her.

Amy opened her eyes, blinked and then drew away.

Wade stopped his hand in mid-motion and pulled it back. "I thought you were fainting."

"No," she said, but she still didn't look at him.

"Sick?" he asked.

She didn't say anything this time. She just stood there, her face pale and drawn.

Wade figured that only left one possibility for the way she looked. "You're not scared of me, are you? Is that what this is about?"

Amy looked at him then, her eyes dark circles of weariness in her white face. "I was trying to check my forehead to see if I have a fever. But now that you mention it, I should be worried. I'm the only one who even knows your mother thinks you did it. I could be in danger."

Wade just stared at her. "You watch too much television."

Amy got a stubborn look on her face that he recognized all too well. At least it added some color to her cheeks.

"Well, when a man makes you promise not to repeat anything you might hear at his place, you begin to wonder." Her voice was rising, and her temper was building. "You said not to tell anyone. Did you mean the county sheriff's department? Are they the ones I'm not supposed to tell what I heard?"

"No," Wade said, doing his best to look her in the eye and trying to be patient. "Of course not."

"Well, just so you know, I'm going to keep my word." She looked him squarely in the eyes, even though she still seemed upset. "For now, anyway. I'm not going to say anything about what I overheard."

Amy crossed her arms and clearly wasn't moving. If he knew her, she'd become more indignant at any moment.

He had to do something, Wade told himself, as he took a step closer and touched her arm. "Come. Let's go tell everyone what you heard. Then it won't be a secret. And we can sit down to dinner and eat our roast in peace."

Amy turned to him. "You're kidding, right?"

"No," he said slowly. Was he missing something? She had sure sounded like she wanted to tell someone the whole, miserable story.

"You can't go out there and announce your mother thinks you could be a murderer—not at Mrs. Hargrove's Sunday dinner. She's using her wedding china and those swans your mother made—they took work. They only have those in fancy hotels."

"The china will be fine." Wade noticed Amy hadn't shaken his hand off her arm. Of course, maybe she didn't realize it was still there. "And the swans are already unfolded anyway so that won't make any difference."

He saw her bite her lip. She always did that when she was undecided about something.

"Like my mother said, the truth is good," Wade coaxed. "Besides, would I be willing to tell anyone what you heard if I really had committed a murder?"

Amy looked at him. "Yes."

He arched an eyebrow in surprise.

"You might think it would confuse me," she said, her voice increasingly firm. Then she scrutinized him with the same look she'd used when they were kids. "I know how your mind works, Wade Stone, so don't think you can trick me."

He grinned. "I wouldn't dream of it."

Then he looked her right in the eye so she would know he meant it. "Scout's honor. I didn't do it."

"You never were a Scout."

"I thought about it. You know that."

He waited, and he could tell from the softness in her eyes that her heart was responding to his plea.

Mrs. Hargrove's kitchen was a simple place. White, ruffled curtains hung at the window over the sink, and a row of jars along the back counter held spices and loose tea. There was no light turned on, and the grayness outside seeped into the room. It wasn't the most romantic place for a kiss, but Wade had waited nine years and he was afraid he might not get another chance.

He moved his hands to Amy's shoulders and gave her a moment to slip away. She kept gazing at him steadily, her eyes starting to look a little damp. But in a good way, he thought.

He didn't ask any questions. He just dipped his head until their lips met. She was warm and yielding but hesitant, enough so that he almost pulled back, until he felt her respond.

From then on, he couldn't have stopped the kiss from deepening if a bulldozer had been headed straight at them. Which, from the pounding in his heart, is what it felt like. He shifted his arms and felt her come further into his embrace.

He didn't know how long they stayed that way. He could hear her breathing—short, little breaths. Then he moved away slightly.

She stared at him, her cheeks pink. "That kiss was a mistake."

"I'm sure it was," he agreed softly but kept his arms around her. He never wanted to let her go.

They stayed that way for a few minutes, him cradling her in his arms as she buried her face in his chest. He thought he might have felt a tear or two through his white shirt. Finally, he bent his head to kiss the part in her hair.

"I'm sorry," he whispered.

She looked up at him.

"I never wanted any of the bad stuff in my family to ever touch you," he said.

"I don't think any family is perfect."

"But the problems in mine are worse than most." He didn't need to say more because she would have read it all in the newspapers at the time. Everybody in Dry Creek had. The abuse. The drunkenness.

She didn't protest further. With that, they separated and turned to go back into the dining room. Things weren't quite like they had been before, though, Wade thought to himself. Amy was holding his hand.

Wade pushed the door open and they walked into the room where the others were sitting.

He noticed his mother's eyes brighten when she saw their linked hands. He gave his head a little shake to warn her not to say anything. He wasn't sure if Amy was helping a friend by holding his hand or if her gesture meant more. And he wasn't going to press her on it. Right now, friendship was a step forward.

"I have an announcement to make," Wade began. All three of the older people had already put down their forks, so they were ready to listen. "Yesterday Amy walked over to my house and—"

Wade stopped to swallow and glanced down at Amy. The words were sticking in his throat. She squeezed his hand and looked back encouragingly.

"The thing is—" Wade started again.

"You're engaged," Charley interrupted in glee. "I knew it. I knew it. You two always were meant to be together. I was just saying that to Edith when we were in the kitchen carving up this roast. Wasn't I, dear?"

"No," Wade said, trying to stop the man. "That's not it."

"Oh," Charley said, his expression deflating. "Well, what else could be important enough to get us all worked up over?"

"Yesterday," Wade began again. He didn't dare look at anyone this time, not at Amy or his mother. He focused on the basket of biscuits on the table. "The thing is that Amy overheard a conversation between my mother and me that would lead anyone hearing it to suppose that I had been the one who killed my father."

Someone gasped. He thought it was Mrs. Hargrove, but it could have been anyone.

Then there was absolute, frozen silence in the room. For a moment, Wade thought the clock on the sideboard had even stopped running, until he realized it probably used a battery so it didn't make a sound, anyway. The wind that had been present earlier grew still, though, and Charley didn't even move enough to blink an eye.

"That's impossible," the man finally said.

"Oh, I assure you, she heard it," Wade responded grimly.

"Well, maybe she heard something," Charley conceded. "What I meant is that you couldn't have done it, because—" The man's voice trailed off as he gave an apologetic glance toward Wade's mother. "I mean, it wasn't the kind of thing two people would have done. Now is it?"

While Charley had been talking, his wife had started patting Wade's mother's hand.

Wade nodded his head. "You're right. It's unlikely to be two people."

"Oh, dear," Mrs. Hargrove said, as though she finally understood. She gave up on his mother's hand and stood up so she could hug her around the shoulders. "I can't believe it. All that time in prison, and you didn't do it."

"She did it for me," Wade said. "She didn't want me to go to jail. Or worse, I suppose."

"But—" Charley sputtered one more

time and then finally shook his head. "If that don't beat all."

It was silent for a moment. Then Wade realized something. "Aren't you going to ask if I did it?"

"Of course you didn't do it," Charley said, but Wade noticed the man wavered a bit. And then he took hold with his usual gruffness. "Well, did you?"

Wade shook his head.

"What I don't understand—" Mrs. Hargrove started to ask a question, but then she stopped.

His mother looked at the older woman and spoke. "It's okay. I'm not sorry I said I did it. Even if I didn't kill anyone. Prison changed me. For the better." Then she smiled up at Mrs. Hargrove. "But you know that. You sent me the Bible, and I started going to the study groups. I found God there."

"But you're innocent," Amy said and left Wade's side to go pat his mother on the shoulder. Mrs. Hargrove moved over to give the younger woman room enough to join her as they stood behind his mother's chair.

Wade rather liked the picture of Amy standing by his mother, even if it did remind him of how difficult it was going to be. "No one knows she's innocent though. We need to find out who killed my father."

"Of course we do," Charley said and then paused. "But it's been almost ten years now. The crime scene is cold. I could ask around among the men, but I'm sure if anyone had seen anything or even had any suspicions that it wasn't Gracie, they would have mentioned it at the time—or later, even. In all those years, it was the biggest thing that ever happened in this town. People still talk about it from time to time. I've never heard anyone say she might not have done it."

"We need to report what we know to Sheriff Wall, of course," Mrs. Hargrove added. "First thing Monday morning. This is something for the county sheriff's department to figure out."

"They're the ones who arrested Gracie the first time," Charley said indignantly. "They didn't get it right then, what makes us think they'll get it right now."

"But you can't blame the sheriff's department," Wade's mother said. "I confessed. I didn't want them poking around and finding any evidence."

"Whoever did it will make a mistake eventually," Amy said as she stepped away from Wade's mother a little. "We just need to recognize it when they do."

The room was quiet. There didn't seem to be much to say to that statement. Wade was very aware that she wasn't meeting his gaze. She could be thinking he would be the one to make the mistake, showing his mother had been right.

Amy stood there a moment and then walked back to the bench and sat down on it.

She hesitated, but she finally slid over. Then she looked up at Wade. "There's room for you here, too. If you want to sit down."

Wade nodded.

Amy watched him. She'd been telling herself that she didn't know Wade well enough anymore to know if he would murder someone. But then she realized it wasn't the Wade of today who was in question. It was her old friend, the Wade she had known as a child, who was standing accused. She'd known that Wade better than she'd known anyone before or since. His heart had been good; she'd have trusted him with her life.

Besides, she'd known when he'd lied as a boy. He didn't do it often, but sometimes he wouldn't tell her how he'd gotten a bruise on his arm or a scratch on his face. She thought he was having adventures without her. Later, she knew he'd been ashamed of his father. Wade had cause to be upset with the man. But she could not believe he had done something so terrible as to kill him.

She thought Wade might say something, but he didn't. He just walked over and slid onto the bench next to her. There was no more room for the two of them this time than there had been last time. Wade's left arm still touched her right arm, and she was still pressed to the wall. But instead of making her anxious, she found it comforting this time.

"I'm afraid the food isn't as hot as it was," Mrs. Hargrove apologized as she sat back down in her chair and gave Amy an approving nod. "But it should still be fine. And I'm sure we're all hungry enough that we'd rather not put it back in the oven and wait for it to warm up."

Amy murmured in agreement with everyone else. She was surprised to realize that she did have an appetite.

"I wouldn't mind saying grace again,"

Charley added, and they all bowed their heads willingly.

"Father, we are truly grateful to You for bringing us together today," he said, his voice gruff with emotion. "Bless this food to our bodies and give us wisdom in what we should do about this whole situation with Gracie and Wade. I'm not about to tell You what to do, Lord, but if You could help us figure out this puzzle, we'd be mighty grateful. I know You have a purpose for us in this, so help us to appreciate that, too. In Jesus' name. Amen."

After the prayer, Mrs. Hargrove picked up the platter of pot roast and passed it to Gracie saying, "Take all you want, dear. There's plenty more in the kitchen."

They were all silent as they passed the food around and then started to eat, but it wasn't an awkward silence. Everyone seemed to be thinking, and Amy guessed that they were all going back to their memories of the time of the murder, wondering if they had overlooked some kind of a clue.

She glanced over at Wade. She hoped he never knew, but the biggest thing in her mind during that time was wondering if he was old enough to marry her. She had actually thought he would stay in Dry Creek and work his family's ranch with his brothers. She had pictured herself bringing them casseroles at the end of a hard day and smiling up at Wade, encouraging him like a wife would do.

She wondered if her face was red, so she quickly looked over at Mrs. Hargrove. "Everything is delicious."

The older woman nodded back. "Thanks."

Amy realized she had no idea back then how ill-prepared she would have been to be a rancher's wife.

Finally, Gracie looked over at her. "You never did hire a ranch hand, did you?"

Amy shook her head. "We talked about it, but money is tight and my aunt was so opposed. She didn't want some strange man lurking around, she said. I advertised for a woman, but we never had any takers on that."

Gracie laid down her fork and leaned closer to Amy. "I've often thought your aunt might have noticed something. I haven't asked her, because I was worried she might have seen Wade do something, but now I wonder if she saw anyone else. I know she used to wave to us from your porch around the time it probably happened."

Amy nodded. "I can ask her."

She wasn't sure what her aunt would say, but Amy felt good to have something to do.

Her family had their own crisis soon after the Stone family had theirs. Maybe that's why her dreams about Wade seemed so real. Her grandfather's senility had begun with vivid nightmares, which woke him up screaming. Her aunt would be up half the night calming him and then she became ill.

By the time Amy was sixteen, she was in charge of the ranch. She didn't know it at first. And she wasn't legally in charge, of course, but everything fell to her. Neither her aunt nor grandfather seemed to have any interest in the animals or the fields. If she didn't do something, no one did.

They finished the meal in silence. Even Charley seemed subdued.

Finally, when it seemed she couldn't bear thinking about Gracie's lost years and Wade's possible actions any longer, Charley remembered why he had invited her to dinner.

"I wanted to show you the elf sketch I made with the new hat," he said. By then, Mrs. Hargrove and Gracie had started clearing the plates off the table. "That way you can make any changes before you come tomorrow. We should talk about it before we paint it."

"Oh." Amy remembered. "My pickup is still not working. I'm not sure when—"

"That reminds me," Charley said. "My nephew, Conrad, towed it over to his station. Just to keep it out of the snow. No charge."

Wade shifted on the bench and looked at Charley. "I hope he doesn't mind if I go over in the morning and put in the starter. I ordered the part from him already."

Charley nodded. "He's probably expecting you to come in then. It doesn't take much to switch out starters."

Wade turned to Amy. "If you need a ride into town, I'm happy to stop by and get you on my way. That way I can fix everything when you're here at Charley's, and I can bring the pickup over when I'm done."

Amy nodded.

"I'll be by your place around seven-thirty, then, if that's all right?"

"That's good." She owed him so she continued. "I'm sorry about what my aunt said yesterday. My grandfather, too. I'll talk to them and be sure they're more welcoming next time."

"Don't." Wade shrugged. "They're entitled to their opinions. I'm sure they won't be the only ones who think you're foolish to even sit here at dinner with my mother or me."

Mrs. Hargrove came into the room again as Wade was speaking.

"I'm glad you're both helping Charley with the sleigh this year," the older woman said as she picked up the empty bread basket off the table. "Shawn offered to help, but he wanted to put a sign on the sleigh, and Charley thought that was a bad idea."

"Let me guess," Wade said with a grin. "'Vote for Shawn for State Legislature.'"

Amy winced, but she had no doubt that's what the sign would have said. "He just really wants to win at something."

"We told him the children who see the sleigh are too young for politics," Mrs.

Hargrove said as she picked up the napkins, too. "And they'd forget to tell their parents. We can barely get the kids to remember their mittens when they leave Sunday school. Even the candy canes Shawn promised to give them wouldn't have changed their memories."

"Well, he's got my vote," Wade said.

"You don't even live here," Amy gasped.

"I might if he gave me a candy cane," Wade teased as he turned to her and winked. "A man's got to live somewhere."

Wade had never winked at her before. Never. He'd frowned. Scowled. Grinned. Smiled. But never once had he winked. It made him look rather rakish, she decided. Playful, even. Handsome, definitely.

"You'd move back?" Mrs. Hargrove asked, her face beaming. "Oh, your mother would love that. I know she wants all of you boys to come home."

"She's already written the letters asking

all of us," Wade agreed. "But with everything that's happening—"

The moment of fun was gone. Wade's face was serious now.

Amy's heart sank. Seeing the difference in him reminded her he could turn the charm on and off. This was a new side to him she didn't know. And, hard as it was, she had to ask herself why he was charming now. Was he trying to distract everyone from the question they all needed to consider? Was he hoping she would remember the fondness she'd felt toward him in their childhood and decide not to tell the authorities about his mother's words?

"Well, I better go see Charley about those elf drawings." She didn't like the suspicions that crowded her mind. She thought she had made up her mind to trust Wade, but apparently she wasn't as sure as she wanted to be.

Wade slid off the bench so she could leave the table. "And I should take my mother home." He looked right at Amy. "I can give you a ride home, if you'd like."

She swallowed as she stood up. "I think Charley and I will be a while. And he already offered to take me home."

Wade nodded like he understood more than she'd said. "Well, I'll pick you up tomorrow morning on my way into Dry Creek, then, if that's what you still want?"

She was silent a moment too long, standing there by the edge of the table as Mrs. Hargrove gathered up the silverware.

"Amy," Wade finally said softly.

She had no choice but to look at him. His eyes searched hers.

"I don't want to pressure you," he murmured. "Make sure you tell your aunt what you heard."

"But she'll—"

"Tell her. You'll feel better," Wade insisted. "I have nothing to hide."

Amy felt her heart lift a little. "I'll be

ready to go tomorrow morning when you come."

"Good." Wade smiled. "It's a date. I'll look forward to seeing you."

And with that, he walked out of the room, leaving Amy and Mrs. Hargrove standing there. It was unfair, Amy thought, that his absence should make the room colder. And that the whistle of the wind should seem louder than it had been. Or that her heart felt such wistfulness when he'd said it was a date.

"I—" She turned to her old Sunday school teacher without even knowing how to ask what she needed to know. "I—" She took a deep breath and did the best she could. "Do you think he could have done it?"

Mrs. Hargrove looked at her for a moment, her face full of sympathy, and then held out her arms.

Amy went right into them. Maybe it wasn't the older woman who needed to answer that particular question. Amy needed to know the truth of it in her heart. Unless she was completely convinced Wade was innocent, she would never trust him enough to—she stopped herself. She should not even be thinking of a future with him. There were so many problems, she wasn't sure God could even sort them all out. Besides, the man might not even be staying around.

Chapter Six

Wade never thought he'd go looking for Shawn Garrett, but he was driving into Dry Creek to do just that. It was almost eight o'clock Monday morning, and before Wade started working on Amy's pickup, he needed to settle a few things with the other man.

In the meantime, he was fretting so much he barely noticed the frost that edged the windows of his pickup. He didn't pay much attention to the bumps in the road, either. He slowed down as he entered the town, but that was only so he didn't disturb any of the tire tracks. Snow covered all of the hard, gray dirt he'd seen yesterday, and snow drifts were forming at the edge of the asphalt. But the tracks were clear, and most of them led to just one place—the café.

Shawn would be there. He was sure of it.

A dozen pickups had already pulled in as close to the café as they could get, so Wade parked along the opposite side of the road, far enough back that he wouldn't be blocking another vehicle. Then he pushed his Stetson hat as far down on his head as he could and stepped out of his cab. He hurried across the road to the café. Ice crunched beneath his leather boots, and the wind blew his breath around until it made white streams in front of his face.

When he stepped up on the porch, he paused for a minute—the same way he did before he slid down the chute for a championship ride. If he'd ever been a praying man, this would be his moment to do so. Winning required focus, and he gathered his resolve around him before brushing the snow off his coat.

When he opened the door, it was with a full swing of his arm, almost daring anyone to slow him down with any kind of a greeting, even a friendly one. He was ready to ride whatever trouble he found.

The light inside wasn't bright, but Wade could see everything he needed as he closed the door behind him. A good-size group of men, mostly retired ranchers by the look of them, were huddled together at a large table in the back with white mugs of coffee in front of them. No one was drinking anything, so he knew they were intent on something. He didn't have time to wonder what it was, though, because he saw who he wanted.

Shawn was sitting in the middle of the café, looking like he was ready to elect himself the grand marshal of whatever parade might be stumbling by. He had an open, leather briefcase in front of him and was flipping through tabbed folders and pulling out glossy, printed sheets like they were important. Not that there was much room to spread his papers out, but he was trying. He was saying something and pointing to what looked like a chart.

Two ranch hands sat at the table with him, but they were paying more attention to the huge platters of ham and eggs in front of them than to the papers. Wade guessed the food was provided by Shawn so he would have an audience for whatever he was peddling.

Wade didn't have enough patience to wait for Shawn to finish the pitch he was making. So he walked over to the table, planted his feet far enough apart to keep his balance if it came to a fight, and spoke his piece. "It's time we had this out, Garrett."

Shawn looked up. His mouth dropped open. "Wade Stone—are you talking to me?"

"Sure am."

"Okay." Shawn stood up and made a great show of removing the paper napkin from where he'd tucked it into the front of his white shirt. He'd already polished off his own plate of breakfast, if that spot of pancake syrup on his shirt was any indication. "You know, I figured you would be coming to town. That's why I'm ready for you." He started rolling up the sleeves of his shirt. "You never could leave well enough alone."

"I've left things well enough alone for years," Wade said. "You're the one telling everyone what to do these days. Changing people's plans like you're in charge of the world."

A flicker of something raced through Shawn's eyes, and Wade figured the man was finally realizing he might be guilty. Or at least in trouble.

Wade took his coat off and threw it on a nearby chair. Then he started rolling up some sleeves of his own. "I just came from the Mitchells—I expected to see

Amy there, waiting for me to take her into town like we agreed."

Shawn grunted in acknowledgment, even though his eyes were beginning to dart around the room like a hamster looking for an escape from his cage.

"I was only doing it for Amy," Shawn finally said, starting to hunch his shoulders in a fighting stance of some kind. "I thought she needed a ride."

"Did she say that?"

Shawn took a step backward and his voice picked up a whine. "That old man said he'd drive her here in that rundown Jeep of his if I didn't take her with me to town. He probably would have crashed into a snow bank, as bad as his driving is. And that vehicle of his has been around since the Wright brothers. The thing could have fallen apart just from the rattling it does. The two of them could have frozen to death in a ditch someplace. It's cold out there. I practically saved their lives."

Shawn ended with a self-righteous look on his face.

"That old man is Mr. Mitchell to you." Wade didn't know why he cared what Shawn called Amy's grandfather, but there it was. "The whole family deserves respect. They've had a hard time of it."

The other man snorted. "Who are you now? The name police?"

Wade looked at the man.

Shawn seemed to realize he might have really annoyed Wade and took a second step back, bumping into the table.

Wade didn't answer right away because he saw the two ranch hands stand up. But when they picked up their plates, he realized he didn't have to worry about them. They were just taking their breakfast to a table that wasn't likely to tip over from all the bumping around Shawn was doing.

"I'm their neighbor—and I aim to look out for them if I can," Wade said. That was a conversation better left to another day. Instead, he zeroed in on the important thing. "You've had your eye on Amy ever since we were kids."

Shawn glanced over at the two men who had left the table. Then he leaned forward as if he didn't want to but felt he had to, just in case anyone was watching. His voice got louder. "And what if I have been after her? You haven't been around to do anything about it."

"I'm here now," Wade said, leaning forward a little himself.

Shawn grunted and seemed bolder. "Yeah, right. For how long? I'm here for Amy, and you're not. If she wants me to take her someplace, I will."

"You never did answer my question. Did Amy ask to come to town with you? It wasn't you twisting her arm?"

Shawn started to say something sharp in response, but then he hesitated and looked at the floor. He seemed a little deflated; his voice was certainly quieter.

"The truth is, she didn't ask me directly," he finally said. "Near as I can tell, her family told her you'd called when she was out doing chores and said you had better things to do today—then they called me saying she needed a ride."

Wade looked over at Shawn, but the words had already taken the fight right out of him. He should have known. "It was Aunt Tilly's doing then."

"I expect so," Shawn agreed. "I don't think Amy was too pleased about it—if she knew about it. She didn't say much as I took her to Charley's."

Suddenly Shawn's eyes widened as he looked past Wade to the back of the café. "I think we better sit down." He had a half-panicked look on his face. "Now— sit down now—that would be good."

Wade knew trouble when he heard it in a man's voice, so he pulled a chair out and did like Shawn suggested. Only then did he look back and see what was happening to cause that reaction in the other man.

All of those retired ranchers were standing up, some of them clearly ready to hoist up chairs and use them in a fight. A couple of them had canes that looked pretty deadly. And one of them even had a cell phone to his ear. Probably talking to Sheriff Wall.

All of them were glaring at Wade.

"Thanks," he said softly to Shawn as he leaned across the table. "They're ready to take me on. I didn't know you were so dear to folks' hearts around here."

"I'm not," Shawn admitted wryly. For the first time since they'd started talking, he looked like the guy Wade had known in school. By now, his hair had gotten messed up, and the gel in it made it stick out at odd angles. His face was a little homely but not bad, once his color had come back.

"If I was dear to their hearts," Shawn continued, his eyes meeting Wade's, "I wouldn't need to keep buying breakfast for the men. I'm hoping they'll vote for me because of it."

"So you're buying votes?" Wade asked,

resisting the urge to pretend to be outraged. "Isn't that illegal?"

"Very funny," Shawn said and then gave a shrug as he rolled his sleeves back down and buttoned them. "Besides, it's only ham and eggs. I'm beginning to wonder if it's even going to work. I'm thinking I should put on a big barbecue dinner. Pork ribs. Corn on the cob. Coleslaw. Maybe even get Mrs. Hargrove to make me some of her biscuits. I'd get the female vote that way."

"Everyone likes those biscuits," Wade agreed. He was watching the men in the back as they sat down again at their tables. The café owner, Linda, came out of the kitchen about then with a pot of coffee and began to pour it into their cups so that should keep them quiet.

"Are they always this unfriendly?" Wade asked as he dipped his head toward the back of the café. "What's got them so upset?"

Shawn was silent for a moment, then he said, "They think you did it."

"Ah." Wade nodded. The day was just full of surprises. "Word spread fast. I didn't expect people to hear so soon."

Shawn nodded. "Charley came in earlier, asking the men if they could remember any strangers in town about that time." It was clear Shawn felt no need to say which time he meant. "I heard about it when I stepped in the door this morning. And I could tell the men had already discussed it in depth. Not that they were finished with it when I came. I only got two takers for my free breakfast, and usually I have six or seven. I even offered a full ham slice instead of bacon—even though it's fifty cents more on the menu."

Wade looked at the man closely. Until yesterday in church, they hadn't seen each other for nine years. Neither one of them had been at their best in high school. They weren't friends, but they hadn't been enemies, either. It was hard to be angry at a man so worried about the price of ham.

"It's not easy to compete with murder when you want someone's attention," Shawn finally finished his complaint, and then he was silent.

"So what's your verdict?" Wade asked. "About me and the murder, that is."

Shawn took his time gathering up the folders on the table and stacking them in a neat pile. Then he frowned slightly like he was trying to look judicial. "Not guilty."

Wade was surprised. "Really?"

Shawn nodded. "Sure."

Something wasn't right, Wade told himself. "Wait a minute. That's too easy. You're just saying that because you want my vote."

"You're going to vote?" Shawn snapped to attention and reached for the top folder. "I can give you my position statement on local issues."

"I'm impressed you have a statement,"

Wade said with a smile. He had to admire a persistent man, even if he was an annoying one. Besides, it wasn't Shawn's fault that the old ranchers were suspicious. "If you want my vote, though, you have to work for it. Tell me why you think I didn't do it. Lack of motive? Opportunity? Couldn't lift the shovel? Some alibi I didn't know about? What is it?"

"Oh, I think you *could* have done it," Shawn answered, a little too easily in Wade's opinion. "And you had motive and opportunity. No question about that. And no one knows for sure where you were at the time. I heard you said you were sleeping in your room, but that can't be proved."

Wade tried not to be disappointed. "Don't tell me you consulted a psychic or something weird like that, and they said I was in the clear. That stuff is mostly bogus."

Shawn tapped his head against his head. "No, I used pure reason."

"That's it?"

"I'm just looking at it from a different angle than most. I'm not basing my opinion on the murder. I'm looking at the cheating angle instead. I remember that all through school, you were always a straight arrow when it came to playing fair. You never cheated on a single test, even when you knew you'd fail. If you had killed anyone, you never would have let someone else serve the time for you, especially not your mother."

Wade was stunned. "You're right! That's it! That's my defense."

"Well, don't tell anyone I was the one to say anything," Shawn muttered with a frown. "And keep it down. I'm trying to get these people to vote for me, and I don't want to appear soft on crime."

"Does that matter in the legislature? It's not like you're running for county sheriff."

Shawn nodded. "Making the laws is right up there next to catching criminals."

"For Pete's sake, don't mention criminals until I leave," Wade said as he gave another look at the men in the back. They were a little too quiet for his comfort. "The posse back there hasn't decided what to do about me yet."

Shawn reached into his briefcase and came out with a white, round button that said Vote for Garrett in bright red letters.

"Here, put this on before you go," Shawn said as he held it out to Wade. "It'll make you blend in."

"Blend in? How?" Wade demanded to know, but he took the button anyway.

"They'll think you're a good citizen if you look like you're going to vote," the other man said. "Especially if you're going to vote for me. I'm the hometown candidate. Whether they like me or not, they have to support me. I promised to get them a bridge if they send me to Helena."

"What bridge? The biggest stream we have is the old Big Dry Creek. And it doesn't carry enough water to need a bridge, even in the spring."

"We haven't got the location yet, but we'd like a bridge. Every place needs one. It draws tourists to the area."

Wade shook his head, but he pinned the campaign button to his coat, anyway. "You owe me, Garrett."

Shawn smiled. "I'll send you an invite to the barbecue when I get it organized."

Wade nodded as he stood up. "You do that."

The sky outside had become more overcast while Wade was inside the café and he took a moment to pull up the collar on his coat and get the leather gloves out of his pocket as he stood just inside the door.

"Wade," Shawn called to him from the table.

He turned to look at the other man.

"I never thought you'd come back."

"Yeah, well, I'm here," Wade said as he turned to leave.

This time he'd actually reached for

the door handle before Shawn called out again.

"Wait," Shawn said.

Wade looked over his shoulder. "What now?"

"Just don't make her care for you again, unless you're going to do something about it this time," Shawn said, his voice loud enough to carry to where Wade stood without catching the attention of the men in the back.

Wade took a step closer to the table. "I thought she was halfway engaged to you."

Shawn shrugged. "I suppose that's true. I'm the half that wants to get married, though. I'm not so sure about her half of things. You know what I mean?"

Wade nodded. He was starting to like his old classmate better all the time. "Thanks for telling me. I'm just not—"

He stopped himself. Whatever troubles he had, it was not the other man's worry. The truth was that he didn't have a future to offer Amy, not unless he figured out what had happened nine years ago. Shawn might believe that he was innocent, but Wade doubted anyone else in Dry Creek had reached that conclusion, including Amy.

There was nothing to do but turn and walk out of the café. By now, the wind had gathered more force, and sharp pieces of icy snow hit his face as he made his way across the road to his pickup. He almost welcomed the sting of the snow.

He was going to stop at Charley's house and find out how they were doing on the sleigh before he went over to the gas station to fix the starter on Amy's pickup. He felt a sudden need to reassure himself that Amy was still talking to him, even if she wasn't sure if he was innocent.

He drove his pickup as close as he could to the gated walk of Mrs. Hargrove's house. Fortunately, there were plenty of places to park. Unfortunately, one of those places was already occupied by a very official-looking sheriff's car.

This can't be good, he thought to himself.

Inside Charley's workshop, Amy kept stuttering. It was chilly, and the sheriff didn't seem inclined to leave anytime soon. He had already asked her what she'd heard at the Stone ranch the other day, and she'd done her best to repeat it to him. But then he wanted to know about the expressions on everyone's faces.

"You were saying Wade looked concerned." Sheriff Wall had raised his pen to write in that notebook of his. The wind was rattling the windows in Charley's workshop. But outside of that, the room felt so quiet, Amy thought she could hear her heart beating.

"He was concerned about his mother," she said as she looked down at the concrete floor. "I didn't mean he was feeling anxious about himself."

The sheriff sighed. "I'm sure you can remember more if you put your mind to it."

"No badgering the witness," Charley growled from where he lay on a tarp, his hands raised to tighten some bolts on the steel runners beneath the sleigh. The smell of turpentine filled his workshop. They'd had the door open when they'd started to repaint the elves on the sleigh, but the sheriff had closed it when he'd come inside.

Amy wondered if she should open it, so they could all breathe better, but she was afraid that would only encourage the sheriff to stay longer.

"That badgering stuff is in a trial," Sheriff Wall said, with a glance down at Charley. "I'm just trying to say she could be more cooperative if she wanted. Women notice things. You know, was he sweating, even though it was cold? That kind of thing."

"His hair seemed a little thicker than

I remember it," Amy said obediently. "And he's filled out quite a bit since high school."

Charley chuckled as he shoved himself out from under the sled. "He's a handsome man. Any woman with eyes in her head can see that."

"That's not what I meant, and you know it," Sheriff Wall snapped as Charley stood. "What I'm trying to get at is—did he look guilty when his mother said he'd done it?"

"He seemed surprised," Amy offered.

"Okay." The sheriff poised his pen again. "We're getting somewhere. What made you think he was surprised?"

Amy considered her words. "His eyes sort of went dark. I mean normally they're brown. Sometimes they turn a little golden—you know, when he's—" Amy stopped. She could hardly say they had yellow streaks when he wanted to kiss her. At least, she thought that's how his eyes were then. She looked down at the concrete again. "Anyway, they went almost completely black. Like he was shocked at what he'd heard."

The sheriff was still studying her when she lifted her eyes.

"You don't believe me?" she asked, not because there was any doubt about the fact. He clearly didn't. But she thought she should protest in some fashion. She could hardly say that she'd been a little shocked, too.

A knock sounded at the workshop door, and Charley started to walk over to answer it.

"It's not that," the sheriff said as he put his pen back in his shirt pocket and folded up his notebook. "I just think you're protecting him in some way. Most folks would be adding details to the story. He said this, or he said that. I'd be having a hard time getting them to stop. But you're not telling me anything but what you heard. Just those few words. And I wouldn't have known about them at all if I hadn't heard the men over at the café talking about it earlier this morning."

"I was going to tell you," Amy said wearily as she heard Charley open the door. "I just hadn't gotten around to it yet. Charley and I have been painting the elves."

"See?" the sheriff said as though she had just proven his point. "Most people would report information about a murder first thing, even before breakfast."

Charley cleared his throat, and Amy turned to see who was there with him.

"He shouldn't be here." Amy said the first thing that came to her mind. She didn't want to see Wade get arrested, especially not if it was because of those few words she'd overheard the other day.

She turned to the sheriff. "He said he was going to fix the starter on my pickup. That's why he's in town. He wouldn't be doing that if he was a murderer, now would he?"

"I'm not ready to arrest anyone yet,"

the sheriff said as he took a step closer to the door where Wade and Charley stood. "I'm gathering information though, and until then—" he looked right at Wade "—I'd suggest you stay in town, young man."

Wade smiled slightly. "I'll be here. I'm planning to drive the Christmas sleigh on Wednesday night."

"Oh." The sheriff seemed a little startled by that.

"He'll do a fine job of it, too," Charley said in a hearty voice. "I think we'll be swinging by your place on the sleigh with a little something for those kids of yours."

"Good. They look forward to that sleigh every year." The sheriff stood there for a minute. "Well, I guess I'll be going, then. Have a good day."

"Same to you," Charley said as he ushered the lawman out.

Charley was going to walk the sheriff to his car. Amy knew that as surely as she knew that all of the elf hats were now green. The older man clearly believed that romance flourished when two people were thrown together.

Amy wasn't so sure that was the case here. She had been more wide-eyed in love with Wade when she hadn't seen him for years than she was now. For them, time spent together just seemed to show up all the problems. Not that it lessened her feelings, unfortunately.

"I hope you told him everything," Wade said as he took a couple more steps into the shop. "I don't want you to be in trouble for not being absolutely candid."

"He wanted to know what your eyes looked like."

"What?"

"To know if you seemed guilty," Amy explained. The inside of the shop was fairly dark, but she still noticed the golden flecks in Wade's eyes. He didn't look like he had kissing on his mind, though. She wondered if that look in his eyes also meant he was worried.

"Just tell him whatever he wants to know," Wade said. "I haven't got anything to hide."

Amy nodded, feeling miserable. "I just wish somebody else had heard your mother say what she did."

Wade nodded. "Me, too."

"The sheriff thought I was holding something back to protect you."

"You don't want to do that."

Amy shrugged. What she wanted was for Wade to be proven innocent, but she wasn't sure that would ever happen. It wasn't like Dry Creek was New York City where there were lab tests and informers the police could rely on. All they had here was Sheriff Wall, and the only murder he'd ever solved was when he'd arrested Gracie. And that wasn't much of a triumph because she'd confessed—and, as it seemed to be turning out, she wasn't even guilty.

Amy looked up when Wade took a few more steps toward her.

"Are you all right?" He lifted up a hand and caressed her cheek.

She shook her head and blinked back a tear. "Yes."

"You're sure?" he asked again.

She shook her head. In the midst of everything, something still hurt. "You stood me up this morning."

"No, no, I didn't," he said as he opened his arms to her.

She went into his arms like a homing pigeon. The wool of his jacket was cold and scratchy, but she liked feeling his arms around her. It made everything better somehow.

"You were gone when I got there," Wade whispered in her ear. "I understand Aunt Tilly may have lied about me calling."

"Oh," Amy breathed.

Wade used his thumb to wipe a stray tear off her cheek. "I would never stand you up."

"Shawn drove me to town instead," she

felt obligated to say. She knew how he felt about the man.

"I know. He's not a bad guy, really." Wade said. "He has some good points."

"But you—" Amy started to protest and then just nodded.

No one seemed to stay the way they used to be, she thought. And the more they changed, the more complicated everything became. She no longer knew what anyone would do, including Wade.

Chapter Seven

The afternoon was almost over by the time Wade left Dry Creek to go home. He'd changed the starter on Amy's pickup, delivered it to her and then gone back to help the owner of the gas station, Conrad Nelson, with some chores to pay him back for the use of his tools. The man had been so happy to help Amy that Wade would have been jealous if he hadn't seen the besotted look on the man's face when he talked with his wife on the telephone.

Wade thought about that look all of the way home.

Before he turned into the drive leading

up to his family's house, Wade saw the other vehicles in the yard. He recognized Amy's pickup with some satisfaction; he was glad she was here.

He barely paid any attention to the older, gray car with the dent in the fender. He didn't know who owned that car, but—whoever it was—he doubted they'd be staying long once he stepped inside the house. The speculations about him should have reached everyone in town by now, and if the men at the café were any indication, public opinion wasn't going to swing in his favor anytime soon.

He parked his pickup on the right side of the barn, where it would be sheltered. Even there, the wind was icy as he stepped down from the cab of his pickup. But he didn't mind. Something about the cold weather suited him these days; maybe he felt he should suffer because his mother had gone to prison to save him from doing so. Granted, he hadn't known what she was doing at the time, but the gesture humbled him in a way nothing else ever had.

Wade hurried to the house and let the screen door slam behind him as he entered the enclosed porch. He took his gloves off and rubbed his hands together to warm them. The door slam should give everyone notice that he was here. He'd wait a minute to give anyone inside time to say their goodbyes and slip out the front door.

Of course, people being the way they were, they'd probably want to tell everyone they'd seen him and maybe even had a chance to scold him a bit. He'd developed a pretty thick skin over the years though. By the time he reached for the knob to the inner door, he figured he was ready for anything.

He was wrong.

When he opened the door, he saw Amy, his mother and Pastor Curtis seated around the kitchen table. They all looked up at him with startled expressions. They obviously hadn't heard him drive in or slam the outside door or anything—and that told him better than words just how completely absorbed they had been in whatever conversation they were having. It was a pure gut feeling that let him know he was the topic of their talk.

"Hi, there." Wade had been around enough drunken cowboys and seen enough guilty faces to have a good idea what was going on, but he figured he'd spell it out to be sure. "This isn't one of those interventions, is it?"

He tried to make it sound like a joke, but it fell flat. The flush on Amy's cheeks gave it away.

Wade noticed his mother's big Bible on the table, its pages open to a section printed in red. His mother had also drawn a heart in the margin of the page in blue ink. A quick look around showed the kitchen floor was spotless, and the dust wiped clean from the cabinets. Someone had been busy while he'd been gone. The light over the table was even working, so the electricity had been turned on.

"We didn't expect you back yet," his mother said, and she gave a good imitation of a smile. "And, of course, it's not an intervention—at least not exactly."

Wade tried to meet Amy's eyes, but by now she was looking down at the table.

"How 'not exactly' is it?" he finally asked.

The table Amy was staring at had been scrubbed until it was spotless. And the air was warm, so the furnace had kept working after he started it this morning. Everything was quite comfortable, but Wade knew what was going on here, and it made him feel cold someplace deep inside. They must want him to turn himself in for his father's murder, and they planned to use the pastor and the Bible to convince him.

"We're concerned about you," his mother began again and then seemed to falter.

"Because we care," Amy added a little too quickly as she glanced up.

He looked at them both and didn't answer. What could he say? He wasn't going to leave Dry Creek until his father's death was settled, but he didn't need to stay in this house. He wondered if Conrad would let him stay in the office of his gas station. Or that shop of Charley's could be shelter for a few nights. He could even curl up in the sleigh if they had finished painting the new hats on the elves.

"We do care," his mother said, this time with more force to her words. "And sometimes it's not easy to tell someone that they need to do something they've never even considered doing before."

Wade nodded. He didn't want to make it easy for them. He'd let them sweat out every word of their request. His mother didn't seem to have anything else to say though, so she sat there, her hand resting on that open Bible like it was her purse and held every dime she had to her name.

It seemed they were at a standstill. Wade didn't move, and neither did the women at the table.

Finally, the pastor spoke. "It's always a free choice to study the Bible. Nobody is going to force you to do it, no matter how much they might want you to—"

"Huh?" Wade asked. This whole thing was getting a little complicated. He stepped over to a chair and sat down at the table with everyone else. "This isn't about me turning myself in to the sheriff?"

His mother gasped. "Of course not."

She even sounded outraged at the suggestion.

Amy lifted her head and stared at him, her blue eyes deepening. "Unless you did do it, then you should follow your conscience."

Wade felt his breath catch deep in his chest and he held Amy's gaze. "You think I did it, don't you?"

Amy flushed pink. "I'm just saying that

if you did, you need to tell Sheriff Wall. We'd stand by you. I want you to know that."

Wade looked at her. She was sincere. He could see that much in her eyes. "I could never ask you to do that. You'd do best to forget about me."

"I already tried that," Amy said and then ducked her head like she wished she hadn't admitted anything. "I mean— we're friends and—of course, I'd write if you were in prison."

Wade's mouth twisted. "Like pen pals?"

The prospect was sour to him. He wasn't sure he'd like to get chatty letters from Amy telling him about her husband and children—and, of course, she would marry, maybe even by spring. If it wasn't Shawn who wed her, then it would be someone else. He couldn't bear hearing about it. But on the other hand, if it was all he could have of her, it would be hard to refuse the crumbs she offered, even if he choked on them.

"I never thought—" He started to speak and couldn't.

Until now, he'd never really pictured what his life would be like if he was arrested and convicted. It hadn't seemed possible that could happen, not even when Sheriff Wall told him not to leave town. There was no evidence he had done anything, but there were so few other plausible explanations.

People liked to have their crimes solved and it was either him or one of his brothers. They were both younger and he wasn't sure either of them could have hit his father that hard. Wade realized he could spend his life in prison. The fact that Amy questioned his innocence meant other people would be even more eager to believe he was guilty.

"They don't really convict innocent people, do they?" Wade turned to the pastor and asked. He knew the answer was yes, but he hoped the man would tell him that it never happened—that Wade had nothing to worry about. He needed some hope.

"Sometimes," the pastor replied softly as he reached out and put his hand on Wade's arm. "Not often, I hope. But—" he looked at Wade's mother "—it happens."

"How did you bear it?" Wade asked as he turned to her.

She was his mother, and early on, he'd stopped picturing her day-to-day life in prison. He sent her birthday cards with little more than his signature. He'd thought she was guilty. It was easier to forget about her than to dwell on what she was facing. "How did you stay sane?"

His mother smiled quietly. "I went willingly. It was much easier, of course, when I learned that I wasn't the first innocent one to be judged guilty and punished for it."

Her hand curled around the Bible on the table, and she drew it closer. "He showed me how to live—really live—no matter the circumstances I found myself in."

Wade nodded. He felt helpless to do anything else. "I'm glad you found your answers."

"Those answers aren't just for me," his mother whispered as she glanced at him. "I want you to know Him, too. I just don't feel that I'm the one to tell you. There's so much I don't know—" She turned and looked at the other man. "Pastor Curtis came over this morning to help me scrub floors, and we got to talking."

Wade felt surprise that the man would want to help his mother clean her house—he always thought of pastors as spending their lives in suits telling people what to do—but he had no time to say anything.

"What she's trying to say is that she'd like me to meet with you," Pastor Curtis added. "Maybe study some of the Bible together. Get to know each other. Talk about God. It's up to you, of course."

Wade's mother slid her Bible closer to

him and left it there for him. He took his Stetson off and set it on an empty chair behind him. He would have done the same in a church. Then he put his hand on the book like his mother had done earlier. He was half-disappointed he felt no sensation. The way his mother treated it, he'd expected a tingle of some sort, at least.

They were all silent for a moment.

"I haven't been to church very often," Wade finally admitted, looking at the pastor. "I'm not sure I would know enough to study the Bible."

"None of us know very much when we start," the man said with a smile. "But I will say this—God doesn't try to hide anything. It's pretty straightforward when you get into it."

Wade looked at his mother. "I'd be willing to try."

It wasn't just for her that he was willing. He needed some answers of his own.

"That's all I ask," she said as she blinked

back tears. She stood up. "I think this calls for some tea."

"I'll heat the water," Amy said as she also stood and then started for the door leading out to the enclosed porch. "It'll just take a minute to get it hot."

Wade watched her hurry out of the kitchen and frowned. No matter what she thought of him, he didn't want any walls between them.

Shadows were starting to form in the enclosed porch as Amy turned on the propane stove. The full kettle was already on the burner because she and Gracie had been planning to have tea when the pastor was here, even before Wade came. The rose-covered china pot was nearby on the card table. Gracie had found the pot several hours ago and washed it in boiling water until it was clean enough to serve the queen, if necessary.

Amy heard the door of the main house open behind her, but she didn't turn around. The wind had blown some snow in through the screens, and her fingers were cold. She hadn't worn gloves out here, but she still picked up the small box of tea Gracie had brought with her. With stiff fingers, she began to search for a few bags that matched. Maybe an orange spice would be good.

The lightbulb hadn't been replaced in the porch light yet and, even though the electricity was on for the house, Amy wasn't ready to climb up on a ladder and change anything at this time of day. Besides, she knew who was on the porch without seeing his face. For one thing, she heard the sounds of his boots stepping across the wood-slat floor toward her. No one walked quite like Wade.

She didn't want to turn around, though.

"I'm sorry," she said, still facing straight ahead. "I know I shouldn't worry about whether or not you're guilty. I should be a goose and just forget it. Or is it the ostrich? The bird with its head in the sand—whichever one that is—that's what I should be."

The footsteps halted before they reached her. She had stopped babbling, and Wade apparently didn't have anything to say, either. The wind still blew and the air on the porch grew colder. It was going to be dark any minute now.

"My parents got this china pot for their wedding," Wade finally said, his voice quiet. "They eloped, and it was the only present they got. My mother's aunt gave it to them. She sent for it all the way from England. Neither one of my parents had much family until they had each other."

Amy turned to watch as he lifted the pot up and examined it.

"It had a crack one time," he added as he set it down carefully. "Right across the bottom. My mother almost cried. But somehow my father fixed it, and it hasn't leaked since. It might be the only thing he did right in his life, but he did that for my mother."

"I didn't know that," Amy murmured. She hadn't realized it would be so chilly out here while she waited for the water to heat. She folded her arms. "It's nice to have some good memories of your father."

"Cold?" Wade asked as he walked closer to her and opened his coat.

She hesitated.

"I don't bite," he said as he grinned. "Not much anyway."

She moved into the warmth, and he wrapped the coat around them both.

Only when she was settled next to his heart did he speak.

"I want you to believe in me, but I don't want you to have your head in the sand," he said softly against her hair. "You're an intelligent woman. I want you to always speak your mind. You don't need to take care of me like that."

They were both silent then. Amy leaned back even farther into his embrace.

"I don't want you to be guilty," she finally said. "I wish I could believe you weren't to blame without knowing any of the facts, just trusting you."

Wade nodded. "It's all right."

The whistle on the kettle sounded and they stepped apart.

"I'll carry the hot water in," Wade offered as they walked over to the propane stove.

Amy nodded. "I'll bring the teapot. The cups are already on the counter."

There was a reason, Amy told herself ten minutes later, that the English were seen as a civilized people. It was the practice of drinking tea. Anyone would find it hard to worry about their problems while they were sipping the warm beverage. It was easier to believe everything would be okay.

No one said much as they drank their tea. It was only when the teapot was almost empty that Gracie said she still wanted to decorate the house for Christmas.

"I know it seems strange," she said as she looked around the table. "But trouble didn't stop the first Christmas from happening in Bethlehem, and I don't want it to stop mine, either."

"Good for you," the pastor said.

"Whatever I can do to help, you just say the word," Wade added.

"If you get us a tree," Gracie turned and said to him, "maybe Amy can help us decorate it."

"I'd be honored," Amy said, and she meant it. Her sack of decorations was still on the enclosed porch. She had shoved it under a small table earlier, so nothing would fall on it. "I have some things that don't go on a tree, too. We could set those around today. I don't have any lights, but I have lots of those old-fashioned bulb ornaments."

"That's just wonderful," Gracie said as she looked around her kitchen with satisfaction. "And the best news is that the pastor here offered to come tomorrow and help me clean up my stove, so I can cook Christmas dinner."

"That I did," Pastor Curtis confirmed and then looked at Wade. "I'm going to enlist my twin boys to help. They're sixteen now, and they'll jump at the chance to scrub anything, if I say they can drive here and back with maybe a side trip along the way. The car's taking a beating, but they're learning."

Wade nodded. "I remember them. Cute kids."

The pastor laughed. "Don't let them hear you say that. They think they're too tough for cute."

Amy leaned back and enjoyed the look on Wade's face as he asked the pastor about his sons. She had never really appreciated all Wade had missed by having a difficult father. A boy needed a man to look up to when he was young. She didn't remember an older man in Wade's life, except for Charley, and they only saw each other because of the sleigh.

When Wade turned to her, his eyes still full of laughter over some story the pastor had told, she wondered why she had never thought about everything from his point of view. If his life had gone on as they'd both expected it to before his father was killed, Wade and she would likely be married now. They'd probably be parents, too. They'd have a son or a daughter, maybe both. They would be sitting at this same table with relatives and children.

Suddenly, the tea didn't seem like enough. If she didn't leave soon, she'd be in tears.

Amy stood up. "I really should be going for today. I have chores to take care of before dark, and I'll be back tomorrow morning bright and early."

"Before you leave," Gracie began, her voice hesitant. "I thought since I'll have my stove ready and the heat and water fixed that maybe you and your family would like to come over for Christmas dinner."

Amy sat back down.

"Like we used to do," Gracie added. "Having Christmas dinner with your family was the one thing Buck let us do to celebrate. I used to look forward to it all year."

"Christmas dinner." Amy repeated the words more to give herself time to think of something to say than because she didn't understand their simple meaning.

"Oh, I'm sure Aunt Tilly—" Wade came to her rescue. "I mean, she's probably got something planned."

"Well, all we can do is invite her," Gracie said with dignity. Then she looked at Amy. "Tell her I plan to have a baked ham and those sweet yams. She'll remember the recipe—she always liked my yams. And then some fresh cranberries and maybe that new green bean casserole if I can find some almonds. Nothing fancy. It's just to be together. She always used to enjoy those times so much."

Amy had forgotten the holidays her family had spent with the Stones. She glanced over at Wade, and he shook his head ever so slightly. He hadn't told Gracie about her aunt—or her grandfather, for that matter, she supposed.

"I think we have some almonds," Amy said for lack of anything better.

"I hope your family can come," Gracie repeated, a shy look on her face. "And tell your aunt not to worry. I know she's been ill so if there's anything she can or can't eat, all she has to do is let me know and I'll work around it."

"She can eat almost anything," Amy said.

Then she saw Wade watching her, his face almost as wistful as his mother's. If she was honest, she felt the same way they both did. Holidays had never been as satisfying after the Stones left. After that, it had been just her aunt and grandfather sitting down to the table and they mostly ate in silence. Maybe dinners like that were always better when shared with more people. Maybe things would work out.

Her aunt had been acting strange though. Amy had told her about the conversation she'd overheard yesterday between Gracie and Wade. She'd expected it to make her aunt happy, but Aunt Tilly had put her hands over her face and ran to her room and cried. Amy had gone to talk to her, but her aunt refused to say anything. Maybe by now though she would have realized there was no reason to avoid the Stone family—not if Gracie was innocent.

"I'll let you know what my aunt says tomorrow," Amy finally said, determined to do her best to reassure her aunt. She didn't know what they would do about her grandfather, but if her aunt was willing to come, they would manage him between the two of them.

Gracie nodded. "We might have apple pie, too, if I can find the time to make one. That's always been Wade's favorite."

"I know," Amy said and couldn't help smiling. "If you don't have time, I'd be happy to bake one for dinner."

"Use lots of cinnamon," Wade said and, when she looked over at him, he grinned. "I'm partial to your pies."

"In that case, I better make two of them," Amy said, feeling pleased with herself as she stood up again. "After I finish cleaning the living room tomorrow, I'll help decorate. But for now, I need to get back before it gets too dark."

Memories of that first apple pie she'd made for Wade kept her happy as she drove home. Life had been so simple that summer when she was thirteen and decided she was in love with him. She'd felt so grown up when she'd baked him a pie. He'd been her hero and her friend.

The lights were on in the house when she pulled into her yard. Enough snow had fallen to cover the tracks she'd made earlier when she'd stopped by to make lunch for her aunt and grandfather. If the snow stayed until Wednesday night, the horses would have an easy time pulling the sleigh, even when all the presents were loaded on it.

It was going to be a good Christmas, Amy told herself. It had been a few years since she'd looked forward to the day this much. Somehow, she'd convince her aunt to have dinner with the Stone family. When she had enough time to think about it, she'd realize that Gracie was no threat to anyone.

Her aunt was sitting at the table when Amy went in the back door and stood in the kitchen, unraveling the wool scarf she'd wrapped around her head.

"You're late coming home for chores." Aunt Tilly stared straight ahead at the window. Usually she had removed the curlers from her hair by now, but they were still on her head. And it looked like she'd sat in that chair most of the day.

"The chickens don't mind," Amy said as she hung her scarf and then her coat on a hook by the door. She had never known her aunt to care much about the time of day; she always claimed schedules were for accountants and school administrators, not for free spirits like her. Amy debated whether she should ask her aunt what was wrong or let her talk about it in her own time.

"Those two goats you have might care though," her aunt said. "They aren't so patient."

"Maybe," Amy admitted. "But they can wait a few minutes."

Amy went over and sat down at the table with her aunt. Only then did Aunt Tilly turn toward her. The older woman hadn't put any color on her face this morning, no lipstick or mascara. That was very unusual. And the buttons on her robe weren't done right.

"You've been crying," Amy said softly as she reached out to put her hand on her aunt's arm. "Are you feeling all right?"

Her aunt nodded. "Never better."

The woman was so brittle, Amy was afraid she'd break.

"Grandpa's okay?"

Her aunt snorted, and Amy was startled. She had never heard her aunt do that before. Then, in a bitter voice Amy barely recognized, the words came from her aunt's mouth. "That old man is always okay. Not that he cares about the trouble he causes other people. We do everything for him, and there he is—always carrying on like he knows what's best for everyone. He doesn't care whose life he ruins."

At least her aunt's anger gave some expression to her face.

"He can be a little overprotective," Amy said as she patted her aunt's shoulder and tried to guess at what her aunt was talking about. "He just gets all riled up at the television. You know he doesn't mean half of what he says. Is he upset about cattle rustlers again?"

Her aunt just sat there, impassive now that her burst of anger had passed.

The room was silent for a minute.

"It might make you feel better to know we have an invitation for Christmas dinner," Amy said, trying to sound positive.

Her aunt looked at her.

"Gracie Stone has invited us—"

"No, absolutely not." Her aunt's voice gained strength, and she stood up and adjusted the collar on her robe. "It's bad enough you're going over there to work. There's no need for us to sit down to eat with them."

"But I told you Gracie is innocent. There's nothing to worry about. And you like the way she makes yams. Remember? The ones she calls her sweetened yams. She's going to make some."

"I told your grandfather about what you told me Gracie said."

"And?"

"Just because she says she didn't do it, that doesn't make it the truth." Aunt Tilly turned to walk away from the table and Amy. "Anybody can say anything. She could be lying."

"I've never known Gracie to lie."

Her aunt turned then, a look of triumph twisting her face. "Well, she had to be lying sometime. First, she said she did it, and now she says she didn't. They can't both be the truth."

"But she confessed to protect Wade." Amy pleaded for reason to take hold with her aunt. "That doesn't make her a bad person."

Her aunt just shook her head. "We can make those yams right here. Gracie gave me the recipe years ago. It's on a piece of paper in the back of one of my old cookbooks."

"But they're our neighbors," Amy said in a final plea.

Her aunt walked right out of the kitchen.

Amy sat there for a good fifteen minutes, hoping her aunt would have a change of heart and come back to say she'd be willing to go to dinner at Gracie's, after all. But nothing changed, except for the sun slipping farther down in the sky.

Finally, Amy looked out the window. If she wanted to do the chores without a flashlight, she'd better get started. It appeared her Christmas wasn't going to be as happy as she had hoped. If it wasn't bitter cold out these days, she'd suggest to Wade that they meet on Christmas Day in their coulee and split one of the apple pies she'd have made by then.

She'd give back every Christmas present she'd ever received if she could have another afternoon with him like the one she'd had at thirteen. It had been enough back then just to be together. The rest of the world hadn't seemed very important.

She sighed, sitting there. Of course, there had been no real reason to worry about anything back then. Justice certainly hadn't weighed on their minds.

It had been a long time since she'd felt so torn in two. She wanted to go to Gracie's—she really wanted to spend Christmas with Wade—but she was obligated to her aunt and grandfather. She was caught between duty and longing.

For the first time, she realized that her aunt and grandfather might not accept Wade, even if he could prove he was innocent of his father's death. Maybe they had such closed minds, they wouldn't even see the truth if they were shown it. What would she do then? Could she bear to stay with her family if it meant never being with Wade? How much did she owe her aunt and grandfather?

Granted, Wade hadn't said anything about a future between them, but he seemed to be putting down roots again, whether he meant to or not. She'd noticed him nailing a loose board back on the side of the barn. And she'd seen the hunger in his eyes when Gracie mentioned her faith.

The Bible talked about honoring your mother and father. Her aunt and grandfather were the closest two people she had. But did she have to give up her future to please them?

Lord. She finally bent her head. *Help me to know what's right in Your eyes. Take my heart and lead me in the way You want me to go.*

Chapter Eight

Wade laid his bedroll out in the barn that night, thinking he'd move into the house later. His mother was in her old room downstairs, but the upstairs still needed some work before anyone could use it. He didn't mind being out here, anyway, not even when it was so cold outside. He just burrowed deeper into his sleeping bag and watched the frost form on the barn windows while he waited for his eyes to close.

The pain in his leg had been subdued during the night and didn't awaken him early like he'd come to expect. He only gradually became aware of the day. He smelled the faint dampness of the old hay that was in the loft before he noticed much else. He hadn't realized there was still hay around, but his father had always insisted on keeping a fair amount of it loose on the floor up there, saying a man never knew when he'd need a nap.

Since his father had added a back door to the barn in those days, allowing him to come and go without anyone from the house seeing him, Wade figured it wasn't napping as much as drinking that his father did in the loft. But no one in the family challenged his pretense; they wanted him to stay out of their way when he was drunk, and the loft was a good distance away.

At some point, Wade figured he should climb the stairs and clear out the empty whiskey bottles, which were no doubt there. And he'd toss the hay onto the ground outside so any animals around could eat it.

Wade didn't want to worry about his father's old bottles on a fine morning like this, though. When he did open his eyes, he lay there and marveled at the way the sunlight filtered in through the window on the east side, making it look like a cross was suspended in the frame. He smiled to himself, wondering if it was a sign like his mother was always claiming to see.

Not that it was a real cross, of course. It was just the way the sun was hitting the normal pieces of dried-out wood that went into making the frame of the window. It did make him think of the Bible the pastor had left with him yesterday, though.

He wouldn't mind seeing a real sign about now. Maybe something like the pastor mentioned on Sunday, with Lazarus being raised up out of his tomb right there in front of his friends. Now, that would have been something. Wade figured anyone would believe in God if he saw that happen.

But to just make up one's mind and decide that from this moment forward, a man would believe in someone he didn't know—that required a pretty big leap of faith.

It took Wade a few minutes, but he realized the thought of making that leap didn't seem as remote as he expected it would. His life had changed in so many ways this past year that he didn't know what he believed anymore. Until his last rodeo ride, he would have said he believed in himself and his ability to win the next championship. He had been proud that he had no need for anyone but himself.

Now, after discovering what his mother had done for him, he wasn't even sure he wanted to go back to the rodeo life. The thrill of winning felt a little hollow. It just wasn't as important as having someone in his life for whom he was willing to sacrifice and who cared about him in return.

His family wasn't much these days, but he wanted to nurture what he had left. His mother had the right idea in asking his brothers to come home.

Wade heard a vehicle drive up to the house and decided he better get dressed. Fortunately, he'd taken a clean shirt out of his duffle bag last night, and it was ready to put on this morning, so it didn't take him long to be ready to go to the house.

When he stepped out of the barn, Wade saw that the pastor's car was there, as well as Amy's pickup. It was Tuesday morning, only two days before Christmas. He'd promised his mother a tree, and he'd have to go looking for one today. There were only scrub pines around, but he might find a tree in the coulee that would stand tall enough to handle ornaments.

Wade walked to the house with his coat flapping around him. He smelled coffee as he walked through the porch area and opened the door leading inside.

He stopped, frozen in place, and forgot to close that same door behind him.

It looked like the circus had come to his mother's kitchen. There might not be any elephants or balloons, but there was enough color to make anyone happy. He felt the chill of the wind at his back and turned around to close the door.

Everything was still there when he looked again, though.

Amy, with a bright blue bandanna around her head, was balancing on an old ladder as she painted a spot of deep red on the side of that old, white shelf above the refrigerator where the bird's nest had been until yesterday. Two gangly, blond teenage boys, with matching orange bandannas around their Mohawk haircuts, were standing on chairs and washing the inside of the window that was above the stove. Pastor Curtis, with some kind of a forest-green, terry-cloth turban on his head, had a paintbrush in his hand and was painting the cupboard knobs a glossy bright yellow.

When Wade had managed to take it all in, he took a step closer to Amy. "Don't tell me that's the ladder from the barn."

He saw a streak of green paint on Amy's right cheek and a bewildering array of colors on what must have been an old T-shirt of her grandfather's. As he looked closer, he saw she even had some purple on the thigh of her frayed jeans. And a spot of bright pink near it.

She cleared her throat.

He realized he'd been staring at her legs a little too long, so he quickly looked up. Only to see her looking down at him with a mischievous smile. "I found the ladder by that old water trough along the north wall of the barn. It was outside. Hope you don't mind if I use it. I had some left-over paint at our place, and when Gracie wanted more color, I brought it over."

Wade had never realized that Amy's blue eyes had a faint hint of purple in their depths. She really was quite enchanting when she smiled.

"Of course I don't mind about the ladder," he hastened to say. "One of the rungs is loose—that's all."

He checked to be sure she wasn't standing on that particular rung. "Tyler fell off that thing the last time anyone used it. Don't step down until I've checked it out. It seems like everything out in the barn was old years ago, and it's all prone to accidents."

His words hung in the air for a moment.

"It couldn't have been an accident with your dad then, could it?" Pastor Curtis finally asked as he looked up from the knob he was painting. "I know the investigation said he was hit with the shovel, but maybe—" His voice trailed off.

"Unless it was raining flat pieces of metal from the sky, I don't see how it could have been," Wade said. "Even an ancient shovel works right when you're hitting someone. It's not like he was on the ladder or anything when it happened."

Which brought Wade back to his immediate concern.

He looked up at Amy. "Why don't you step down for a minute, and I'll see if I can fix the rung on the ladder."

She nodded, obviously a little distracted. "Give me a minute."

Wade didn't want to argue on such a nice morning, but he made sure he was close enough to catch her if she fell.

"I am painting a bird on the side of this shelf," she said as she looked down at Wade. "In honor of the bird's nest that was here. What do you think? Maybe a red Christmas bird? The one you see in pictures. Your mother would probably like that."

"I think that bird's a cardinal. You don't find them around here. I'd guess the nest belonged to a very ordinary sparrow," Wade said. Sometimes he hated to be so practical, but he didn't want the pastor to think he was a man who sugarcoated the truth. "I doubt any exotic birds would come in here to lay their eggs."

"Well, it doesn't matter if they did or not," his mother said as she waltzed into the kitchen with a broom in her hand and looked up. "I told Amy to use her imagination. That's just what this old house needs to bring it alive."

Then his mother turned to Wade and smiled. "It's beginning to feel like home, isn't it?"

Wade looked around and nodded. "All we need is Jake and Tyler living here."

And Amy, he thought, but caught himself before he said anything.

"I'll fix you some breakfast," his mother said. "The pastor brought some muffins."

"My wife, Glory, made them for us this morning," Pastor Curtis said as he looked up, the pride in his eyes obvious. "And I have to say they're good. She never does anything halfway—not even baking. She put frozen raspberries in them, and pure vanilla."

"I'll eat one a little later," Wade said as he put his hand back on the ladder. "I can wait for Amy to finish up."

His mother gave him a nod of approval. "We need to take good care of her."

"I know," Wade said and grinned. "We don't have workman's comp."

"Oh, you," his mother said, and Amy chuckled.

A few minutes later, Amy put the wing feathers on the Christmas bird—a cardinal, she thought a little defiantly—and added a nest to her miniature mural. She had painted the bird's beak open, as if it was in song, even though she didn't know if a cardinal sang or not. It made a happy bird, though, and she liked to think that this mural would be a warm reminder of the holiday in this house for years to come. She even planned to put her initials—very small, of course—in the corner of the picture so she'd be a part of this house, too.

It didn't take her long to finish painting her scene. She heard the Curtis twins doing bird whistles as they scrubbed the old window with vinegar. The pastor had brought out a new window to replace the broken one, and he'd put that in before he'd started working on the cupboard knobs. Gracie had said she wanted more color in her kitchen, and they were working toward that.

Amy turned a bit so she could see the full effect of the changes. Unfortunately, when her weight shifted, she felt the rung beneath her foot give ever so slightly.

"Oops," she said as she felt the rung give even more. She heard the gasps of others as the final crack came. Then she felt herself falling—down, down.

Right into Wade's arms.

"Oh," she breathed in surprise.

"Oh," he said at the same time, relief evident in his voice.

"Are you all right?" Gracie was suddenly there, looking at her with a worried expression on her face. The pastor and the Curtis twins were gathered around as well.

"I've got her," Wade assured everyone, even though it was obvious.

Amy felt like she'd dropped from the sky. She didn't have any pain, but she was shaken up. "I'm fine."

Only then did she realize how safe she felt in the midst of everything. Wade would always catch her. She felt him pull her a little closer as though he was afraid she was still in midair. She felt the strength in his arms and knew she was in no danger.

She looked up to thank him and found herself suddenly shy. His eyes were intense, warm with flashes of yellow in the midst of the brown. His jaw was not yet relaxed, and his mouth was pinched. He'd been worried. She knew he was going to kiss her, even before she felt his lips touch her forehead.

"Don't ever get hurt," he whispered, pulling back enough so that she could see his face again. She could feel him trembling, and she would have promised anything just to reassure him.

"I won't," she heard herself saying, even though no one could ever keep that kind of a pledge.

He gave her a crooked smile, as though he knew how foolish she was to make that commitment.

"Me, too," he added. Then he carefully set her down so that she was standing in front of him.

"We need to make you some tea with honey in it," Gracie said. "For the shock."

Amy turned to the woman and nodded. Everyone had their own way of coping with a crisis. "That would be very nice."

"We'll all have some," Gracie said as she looked over at Pastor Curtis and his sons. "Or maybe some cocoa for the boys?"

"They'd appreciate that," the pastor said as he gave his boys a nod. "Go ahead and clean up so you're ready when Mrs. Stone is."

The twins headed back to pick up the rags they'd been using on the windows.

"I'll start the water," Amy said as she stepped away from Wade. They hadn't cleaned off the regular stove yet, so she'd have to heat the water out on the propane stove. "It'll just take a minute or two."

This time she would leave the teapot in its place of safety in the cupboard until she was ready to fill it with hot water. After learning how much Gracie treasured it, Amy didn't want to take any chances that it might crack again. Everything in life was so fragile.

"I'll take the ladder back to the barn," Wade said as he moved closer to it. He folded the ladder legs together and hooked it over his shoulder. "I don't want any more accidents around here."

Amy nodded. "No one does."

Then she walked over to the door that led to the enclosed porch and opened it.

The bite of the wind made her realize she should have brought her coat out with her, but a minute later Wade was coming out behind her with her coat in his hand. He held it out to her, and she slipped it on.

"Thanks," she said.

"I'm going to see if I can get the covers for these screens to fit tighter," Wade said as he turned to look at the ones behind her. "We can't have you coming out here when it's so cold."

Amy stepped over to where the propane stove was. The kettle was on the shelf near the stove, and a jug of water sat there ready to pour. She busied herself starting the water to heat.

"I don't remember your mother drinking so much tea," she said as she glanced up and saw Wade finishing with the last screen. The wind wasn't blowing into the porch like it had been.

"There. That's better," he said as he

took a step closer to the outside door. "I'm going to go and see if I can find a tree that we can use to decorate."

He reached into his coat pocket and pulled out a bandanna that he then tied around his head. Amy had seen the old-timers around here do that to keep their ears warm in the bitter cold. Once he had the bandanna secured, Wade settled his Stetson firmly on top.

He was still handsome, Amy decided, but in a sort of old-man way.

"Be careful," she said.

He grinned. "Oh, I will be. I want to see what this house looks like when it's all dressed up for Christmas Day."

Amy didn't match his smile. "I should say—I don't know if my aunt will come to dinner."

Wade nodded and his face grew serious. "Because of me?"

"More your mother, I think. I don't suppose the two of them had a fight that we didn't hear about? I don't know what's wrong with my aunt."

"I don't see how they could have. They were doing fine that last Christmas." Wade paused. "I remember your aunt got all dressed up and sang some of her Broadway songs when we finished dinner. She even did a little swirling tap dance. It was fun. And then it all happened so fast—my mom confessed and was in custody almost immediately. There just wasn't any time for a fight. I don't think they even saw each other after that Christmas."

Amy figured she might as well get the problem all out. "My grandfather probably won't come, either. He gets too confused without my aunt, especially if she were to tell him she was refusing to come for some reason. He'd be upset and unpleasant and—well, I did hide the BB gun, but who knows what else he'd do."

Wade nodded. "We'll have to find a way to tell my mother."

"She's so generous to even invite us."

Wade smiled slightly. "You're our neighbors. She wouldn't think of not inviting you."

Amy felt her insides clench. She knew what was coming.

"And you?" Wade asked.

She thought he might look away, but he didn't. He just kept looking at her.

"I'm going to try and time it so I can," she said, not meeting his gaze. "If Gracie will agree to have her dinner around two o'clock. That's when my grandfather and aunt take their naps, and I could slip away for an hour or so and—"

"You'd sneak over?" Wade's voice was quiet. "Without telling them?"

She looked up at him. "Well, I don't know if that's what I'd call it. I figure there's no point in upsetting them, and I would probably be back before they even woke up. That hour is usually pretty quiet at our place."

Amy felt like she was babbling, and

Wade was standing there in silence, letting her.

"I know it's not ideal," she finally confessed.

"I don't think my mother would want to put you in this kind of a situation," Wade said. His face didn't give away his feelings on the matter. "Neither one of us want to make trouble for you at home."

With that, he turned and opened the door to the outside. "Don't wait tea on me. It might take me a bit to find that tree."

Then he very quietly closed the door behind himself.

To Amy, it felt like he was closing the door between them.

The whistle on the tea kettle sounded, and she turned back to the propane stove. She blinked back a few tears. She hoped everyone inside would think the tears came from the chill of the wind and not the confusion in her heart.

Chapter Nine

Wade never made it back for tea—or supper, either. After leaving Amy in the enclosed porch, he walked down to the coulee that bordered the Stone and Mitchell ranches. He needed to be alone for a while.

After he walked some, his heart slowed, and he looked around. This was his first chance to see how the fields of his family's ranch were faring after the years of neglect. The ground was frozen, but he was still able to dig up a small sample of dirt and crumble it in his fingers. The abundance of dead grass and leaves seemed to indicate the soil was fertile. The fences would need fixing if they were to start raising cattle or horses, but his family should be able to plant a crop in the spring, if they could get some of the old equipment working.

He wondered how difficult it would be for them to make a new life on the ranch. They had a few friends here. Mrs. Hargrove and Charley were leaders in this small town and would do all they could to be sure his family was welcomed by others. The pastor and his boys could be counted on their side. And he felt like Conrad at the gas station was a friendly acquaintance, at least.

And there was Amy.

Wade found the tree he was looking for at the bottom of the coulee. Most of the wind that blew through this area didn't hit the low spots, so the pine was straight, even though it was short. Wade had stopped at the barn to pick up a small axe that hung on the inside wall, so it did not take him long to cut down the tree.

As he dragged it up out of the coulee, Wade pondered how often in life people were bent by the strong winds around them. He knew he shouldn't expect Amy to be able to stand against her family when it came to him and his mother, but it still pained him that she couldn't. He had never let himself expect a life with her, but it turned out he was disappointed nonetheless.

The sun was beginning to set when he returned home with the small tree.

"How perfect," his mother said when he brought it in through the kitchen door. "Amy said you'd get the best one. She'll be coming back in the morning to help us decorate it."

He had never seen his mother so excited. He laid the tree along the wall.

"I wonder if we have an old bucket somewhere to set this in," he said.

"Amy might have something we can

use, too. She even has a nativity scene that she's already set up for us," his mother continued, her face beaming. "Come see. It's in the living room on the coffee table."

Wade took off his snowy boots and left them on the rug by the door before following his mother into the other room.

Everything smelled clean in here, too. He guessed it was some kind of lemon polish that made the difference. At one end of the sofa, a lamp was giving a warm glow to the area. A candle was burning in the middle of the coffee table, and several plaster figures were arranged near it.

"I see the shepherds," Wade said as he stepped closer, "and the Baby Jesus."

"Amy says she lost the Mary and Joseph figures years ago," his mother said, and then leaned closer to confide, "I expect as a child, she had a hard time with them, because they were parents. She doesn't remember doing anything to the figures—I asked if she knew where they were—but she might have thrown them away. We learned about things like that in prison. In our sessions."

Wade nodded but didn't comment. He couldn't get used to his mother having had therapy with criminals.

"I was in the domestic violence group," his mother continued as she reached out to gently touch the Baby Jesus. "So many hurting people in that group. I'm still praying for some of them."

They were both silent for a moment. Wade tried to imagine what it would feel like to be able to pray for people he was worried about. To pray for himself, for that matter. To not be alone when he faced his problems.

"I'm glad you're home," Wade finally said. He'd found a list of questions in that Bible the pastor had given him, and he planned to spend some time this afternoon reading the book and trying to answer them.

"I'm glad you're here, too." His mother turned to him and smiled.

Then she lifted up a cloth bag that had been half-hidden from his view by the sofa. "She has lots of other ornaments, too. All from her parents."

His mother opened the bag and carefully took out a red, round ornament. "Look at these. She's kept them all these years."

"I expect they mean a lot to her if they come from her parents," Wade said. "I don't remember her ever talking about them before. It was always her aunt and grandfather who she seemed to care about."

"And not even her grandfather that much in the beginning," his mother reminded him. "It was all Aunt Tilly. That woman gave up everything for Amy—I have to respect her for doing all she could to be a mother to her niece."

Wade nodded, telling himself he needed to remember what Aunt Tilly had done.

They didn't speak much more, and before long, Wade went out to the barn.

He couldn't find a bucket, so he used a couple of boards to make a temporary stand for the tree. After carrying the stand to the porch, he brought the tree out and set it upright in the stand.

He carried it back to the house, and his mother greeted him like he was returning from some war. He knew he should warn her that this fantasy Christmas she was planning wasn't going to be all that she hoped. He could tell that Amy had not talked with her about her difficulties in sharing the day with them. Or the fact that her aunt and grandfather were not coming.

Maybe he could find some other guests, Wade told himself. If he did that, his mother wouldn't be so disappointed. And how hard could it be, he asked himself. Any of the ranch hands around would surely welcome a home-cooked meal for the holiday, whether it was prepared by an ex-con or not. Maybe the pastor would know some people he could ask. And if he talked to the pastor, he could suggest they pray about it. That should get some results.

Amy put on her Christmas earrings the following morning, the ones with the bulbs that lit up as if they were miniature neon lights. It was a beautiful Christmas Eve day, and she was going to the Stones' to help decorate their tree as soon as she finished her chores. She planned to enjoy herself at the neighbors' even if the general mood at her own house wasn't very festive.

At the last minute, when she was dressing, she had added her red sweater with the big, white snowflakes on it. Then she slipped an old, hooded jacket over that before she went to the coat rack in the kitchen and put on the parka she wore when she went out to feed the chickens.

The snow was falling softly, and it was quite the winter wonderland, like the song.

She sang about sleigh bells ringing to the chickens as she scattered their grain around the barn. She wasn't sure, but she thought they noticed her earrings—or maybe they were just looking up at her because of her singing. Regardless, she gave them a little extra feed in honor of the day.

She was still humming Christmas songs when she came in from gathering the eggs. She was pleased to think how easily the runners on the sleigh would move over all the snow this evening.

Charley had told her he was going to park the sleigh behind the old barn where the pageant would be held. Once the last carol was sung inside, he and Wade would bring the sleigh around for people to see as they left the pageant. No one pretended the sleigh was from Santa Claus, but the children liked to see the horses pull it around, anyway.

Amy was surprised to see her aunt

standing at the stove when she came in the back door.

"Be sure and clean your boots," Aunt Tilly said as she turned from what she was doing.

Amy was already unwinding the wool scarf from around her neck. "I always leave my boots by the door." She paused a moment. "Is that bacon I smell?"

"And I'm making you a cheese omelet to go with it," her aunt said, sounding pleased with herself.

As she hung her scarf on the rack, Amy tried to remember the last time her aunt had cooked anything. She made tea for Shawn in the mornings, but that was generally all. Amy baked the muffins they ate.

"I know I've been giving you a hard time lately," her aunt continued as she took a spatula out of the jar on the counter. "So I'm going to try to do better."

"You don't need to do anything." Amy unzipped her parka.

"Yes, I do." Her aunt lifted the corner of the omelet and folded it over.

Then she turned to Amy with a satisfied look on her face. "I've decided to just forget all about those Stones. People like that always have trouble, and we don't need to worry about what they're doing. We've got our own life right here."

Amy didn't say anything for a minute. "They're good people."

"I know. I know." Her aunt waved her hand around in a way that was dismissive of the very thought. "Forget I said anything about them. I'm sure they do the best they can. I know it hasn't been much fun for you lately, here with your grandfather and me. But I've decided that needs to change." Her aunt took a deep breath. "We're going to the pageant tonight."

Amy felt her parka drop to the floor. "What?"

Her aunt hadn't been out of the house for years. She worried about crowds. About the germs, the possible drafts, the noise of the children. She even worried about crime—in Dry Creek—when she had to know it was rare.

Her aunt was still talking. "The doctor said I should do more, and it won't hurt your grandfather to go out, either."

Amy bent down to pick up her parka and hung it on the rack. "When the doctor said you could go out, I think he meant things like visiting a friend. Something quiet. Or maybe going to the café for lunch. But the pageant! There aren't even regular chairs in the barn where they have the pageant. It's mostly bleachers and folding chairs."

"I can stand if I have to," her aunt said as she slid the omelet from the pan onto a waiting platter that had a sprig of parsley already on it.

"It'll be snowy out tonight," Amy persisted as she slipped her boots off. "Even inside the barn, it will be cool. And all the children in the church will be there—you always worry about the flu when you're around little kids."

"I can't live my life in a bubble," her aunt said, as though she did daring things every day.

It was silent for a moment.

"Well, I guess we could take a blanket for you to sit on," Amy said, finally relenting as she stood there in her stockinged feet and wondered when her whole world had turned upside down. "And you always love a good show. They've started having the angel swing from a pulley over the crowd again. It's really something to see."

"I could tell them a thing or two about how to put on a pageant," her aunt said as she carried the platter over to the table.

Amy sat down to the best breakfast she had eaten in months and let her aunt talk about all of the ideas she would use to make the nativity story worthy of Broadway billing if only someone had thought to ask her how it should all be done. One flying angel wasn't enough, she said. The shepherds should have real sheep as well.

"The boys bring in their dogs to play the parts of the sheep," Amy said.

Her aunt clearly disapproved of that. "Animals can't act. A sheep needs to be played by a sheep."

Amy tried to slip in the information that she was going over to the Stones' for the morning while her aunt was so caught up in what was wrong with the pageant. But it didn't work.

"Surely, you don't need to go again," Aunt Tilly said.

"I'm going to help Gracie decorate for Christmas."

"If you wanted to decorate, you could put up some more tinsel on the tree we have."

That stopped Amy. Her aunt insisted on them using her old pink aluminum tree from the fifties, and Amy refused to add tinsel to it. The tree was already dripping with it. If they kept on, they'd be able to use it for a lightning rod.

"It's my job to help Gracie." Amy finally found her footing again in the conversation. "I can't afford to turn down paying work."

"I suppose," her aunt finally agreed as Amy pushed her chair back after breakfast. "But hurry home. I want us to plan the menu for our Christmas dinner tomorrow. I'm thinking Cornish game hens."

Amy stayed sitting. "Oh."

"I know you said Gracie Stone invited us over to eat with them, but that's simply impossible," her aunt said, not looking Amy in the eye.

"I disagree." Amy stood up. "The Stones are back, whether you want them to be or not. There's no way to avoid seeing them. Why, you can stand on the front porch and see them sitting in their yard."

"Nobody is sitting in their yard this time of year."

"I'm just saying, they're close neighbors."

"That doesn't mean we have to talk to them," Aunt Tilly said as she stood also. "No good ever came from being friends with them in the first place."

The room wasn't as warm now that Amy and her aunt were facing each other across the kitchen table. They were both silent as they looked at each other.

"You seem tired," Amy finally said. Her aunt had used too much lipstick, as though she was trying to make herself look more vibrant than she really felt. "We can talk about this later. I need to make some apple pies this afternoon. I promised the Stones I would give them an apple pie, and I plan to do that."

"Well," her aunt said as she stepped away from the table. "I suppose that's fine. It can be seen as charity if nothing else."

"That's not what I'm doing it for," Amy said, but her aunt was already walking out of the room.

Amy stacked the breakfast dishes and washed them as quickly as she could. She wasn't as carefree as she had been when she put her earrings on this morning, but she was still determined to enjoy the day.

The snow wasn't falling quite as heavily when she drove over to the Stone ranch an hour later. She saw tracks in the gravel road that went past both ranches. Pickups—maybe driven by some of the hands from the Elkton ranch—had been by earlier.

When she knocked at the enclosed porch, Gracie called for her to come inside.

Amy smiled when she saw the kitchen again. "It really does look brighter in here."

"You did such a fine job," Gracie said as she stepped closer. "Here, let me take your scarf and coat. We can hang them over here. Wade put in a new rack for us, so there's room for more coats to hang."

Gracie hung Amy's coat up as the younger woman took off her boots.

"Wade says we need extra hooks if we're going to have more people over now. He's out in the barn looking for an extension cord in case we get any lights, but he did the hooks this morning so we'll be ready for Christmas Day."

"Oh." Amy straightened up, even though she only had one boot kicked off. "I'm afraid that with—"

She could hear the outside door opening.

"That must be Wade now," Gracie said as she walked over to the kitchen door and opened it.

Wade walked in from the enclosed porch. Snowflakes were sprinkled on his Stetson and the shoulders of his coat. He pushed his hat back the first thing, and

Amy noticed his eyes. They were, she decided, pleasant. Not warm. Not cold. They greeted her like she was a casual acquaintance—welcome to be sure, but not close enough to stir any deep emotion.

She'd lost him.

"I was just telling Amy that you made these hooks," Gracie said as she pointed to the nice oak rack where she had hung Amy's parka.

"I didn't really make the hooks," Wade said, as he removed his hat and brushed the snow off of it. "All I needed to do was put in a few screws and hang it up. I found the kit in the hall closet."

"Well, still," Amy said, working hard to keep the cheer in her voice. "It takes some work to put anything together."

Wade didn't have much to say to that. He just hung his hat on the rack and then started taking off his coat.

"I was just telling Amy how much I'm looking forward to having guests on

Christmas Day. I know we'll see a lot of our neighbors tonight at the pageant, but—"

"We're going to the pageant?" Wade interrupted to ask his mother. "In Dry Creek?"

"Well, of course," Gracie said. "It's Christmas—we want to acknowledge the birth of our Lord no matter where we are."

Wade looked speechless.

"Besides, you told Charley you were going to drive the sleigh, and that's right after the pageant."

"I guess I could stay outside with the horses."

"Wade Stone, you'll do no such thing," his mother scolded him mildly. "That pageant is practically a church service. You need to be respectful."

"It's actually quite nice," Amy added.

"Everybody goes," his mother said. "And we've never gone once. Besides, it will give us something to talk about when we have Christmas dinner together. Aunt Tilly is going, isn't she? I'm sure she'll have wonderful things to say about it."

Wade looked right at Amy when his mother finished.

"Oh." Amy swallowed. She didn't know how to say her aunt wasn't coming to dinner.

"Amy mentioned earlier that Aunt Tilly probably won't be able to come," Wade said, his voice smooth and calm. "She stays home on holidays nowadays."

Gracie didn't crumble. Her smile didn't fade.

"Aunt Tilly does remember all of the wonderful holidays our families spent together, though," Amy added, to try and make it better.

"Of course," Gracie said, and she looked at Amy.

Amy's heart sank. She'd lost Gracie too. Like Wade, she was looking at Amy much too politely.

"I'll be bringing an apple pie over in the

morning." Amy tried to make everyone happy again. "Extra cinnamon like Wade wants."

"That will be fine, dear," Gracie said with a nod.

No one even asked if Amy would be coming to eat with them by herself. She supposed they were simply being tactful. She had never realized until she stood in Gracie's kitchen that she simply wasn't as tough as either of them.

Wade found an excuse to go back out to the barn, and Amy and Gracie silently put the ornaments on the tree. It wasn't at all like Amy had imagined it would be. There was no reminiscing about past Christmases. No choosing which ornament was anyone's favorite. No teasing about presents that might go under the tree.

When they finished the tree, Gracie took out her checkbook and tallied up the hours Amy had worked.

"You'll want your wages in time for

Christmas," Gracie said as she gave Amy the check.

An hour later, Amy was back at her grandfather's place, getting ready to make the pies. Her aunt was taking a nap, and her grandfather was watching television. Christmas had lost all of its appeal.

She added a little extra cinnamon and sugar to the pies, picturing how much Wade would enjoy them. Then she cut a big heart in each of the top crusts. It wasn't the best symbol for Christmas, but she hoped it showed that she loved Wade—and Gracie, too.

She had just never thought she'd need to make a choice when she loved someone.

Then she heard a sound in the doorway and turned to see Aunt Tilly, standing there in her bathrobe holding a small cardboard box.

"I know you're having a hard time this Christmas," her aunt said with a sympathetic smile. "So I brought out some things I saved for you over the years."

"Oh," Amy said as she wiped her hands on her apron and took a step closer.

The box her aunt held was spotted with water stains and held together with tape. It was obviously old.

"I've kept it in the back of my closet," Aunt Tilly said as she handed over the box. "For when you were older."

Amy carried the box over to the kitchen table and slowly opened the flaps. She was mystified as she pulled away layers of white tissue paper that had aged—and then she saw them. There, in the middle of the crumbled paper, were the two missing figures from her nativity set.

"My Mary and Joseph?"

"Yes."

Amy was bewildered. "But where did they come from?"

"I had them."

"But how—?"

"You seemed to be so taken with them as a child. I was afraid you were getting too attached. I thought they might remind you of your parents, and you'd end up feeling sad if you broke them. So I put them away one Christmas and just didn't take them out when we had the set the next year. It was for your own good."

Amy went absolutely still. "You let me think I'd lost them."

"Well," her aunt said brightly, "they're here now. All safe and sound."

"But I looked all over the house for them. I missed them."

Her aunt didn't answer.

Amy almost couldn't speak any more, and yet she couldn't keep silent either. "How could you do this?"

"They're only plaster figures," her aunt said, her tone dismissing them. "It's not like they're real."

"Like Wade," Amy replied softly, all of the pieces of the puzzle starting to fit together for her. "He's real, but you don't want him around me, either. If you had your way, you'd box him up and hide him away, too. And I suppose you think that's for my own good."

"It *is* for your own good. He'll only hurt you. Not that he can help it. He's a Stone."

They were both silent after that, sitting there looking at each other and further apart than they had ever been.

Finally, Amy decided she didn't have anything more to say, so she stood up and went back to finish her pies. She needed to pray for her aunt, but she couldn't summon up the will to do it yet. In the meantime, she needed to put the pies in the oven to bake.

Her aunt quietly left the kitchen, but Amy barely noticed. She didn't understand how fear could make her aunt do something like that. Maybe she had been too attached to the little plaster figures of Mary and Joseph as a child. Maybe they did represent her own parents in some subconscious part of her. But what did it hurt if she felt their comfort at Christmas? The fact that her aunt feared the future hadn't given her the right to hide the figures away and not even talk to her about it.

The realization was slow in coming, but Amy finally saw it clearly. She was more like her aunt than she'd ever thought possible. She was afraid of being too attached to Wade, too, and it wasn't because he might break. No, she was afraid simply because she didn't have any guarantees in the future if she let herself be close to him again. Would he stay? Would he propose? Would he dance a jig and howl at the moon? She had no idea what the future held with him, none at all.

What she did know was the here and now. She knew her heart warmed every time she saw him. She knew that he was growing closer to her and to God. She knew that she might have a life with him someday.

Then she realized she might have already lost Wade by being too afraid to trust him.

Dear Lord, she prayed. *Help repair the bond between the two of us. Guide us. Please.*

Chapter Ten

It was getting dark when Wade and his mother drove up to the barn that was being used for the pageant. The snow was no longer falling, but it was almost a foot deep in places. Someone had come through with a tractor plow recently and cleared a wide space for parking. No other buildings were close by, but there were some trees beside the barn and their bare branches showed black against the sky.

The night was cold, but the wind was no longer blowing. The lights from the houses in Dry Creek were visible, and a couple of vehicles were driving down the gravel road coming from town to the barn.

Wade hadn't planned to get here this early, but his mother hadn't been sure when the pageant would begin and she didn't want to be late. She was throwing herself into life in Dry Creek with an enthusiasm that made Wade nervous. It made her too vulnerable, but he didn't say anything as he parked his pickup at the far end of the plowed area.

Light was spilling out of the windows of the barn, so Wade knew other people were already inside—probably parents with children who were rehearsing their parts or making changes to their costumes.

He heard a soft gasp and turned to his mother as she sat in the passenger seat. She was pointing at the front of the barn.

"Just look at those murals," his mother said, her voice filled with wonder. "Mrs. Hargrove wrote me about them, but I never pictured anything as fine as this. I understand that the pastor's wife—you remember her, Glory Curtis?"

Wade nodded.

"Well, she and a niece of hers painted them using scaffolds and everything," his mother continued. "Amy helped when she could get away from home, too. In fact, she told me that's where she got some of the paints we used in the kitchen. They had a big meeting and decided to use strong colors to show scenes from the history of this area—they wanted the paint to match the kind of grit the men and women had who settled here. You know, the drought—the depression."

"Well, they did a good job."

With the help of the approaching headlights, Wade could see the colors clearly, and Amy was right. They were vivid yellows and bright reds and deep greens. And what looked like a blue denim sky in an old quilt.

"I wonder—" he said and then paused.

"It's just—if they were painting scenes from today, would they still use the same kind of colors? I haven't noticed much grit around lately."

"Wade Stone." His mother turned and chided him. "You can't just go and give up on people like that—" Then she suddenly stopped. "I'm sorry. It's Amy, isn't it?"

He smiled a little. "How did you learn so much about people in prison?"

"It wasn't because of prison," she said as she lifted up the Bible she'd brought with her. "It was this right here. If you want to understand people, this is the place to go."

Wade nodded. "I've been reading it."

His mother was silent for a moment, and then she asked, "Well?"

"I think you might be right," he said. "It's making sense to me."

"Good."

"I even decided to do like you," Wade said. His mother was listening to him closely. "I asked God to give me a sign to let me know who killed Father."

"Oh." His mother's eyes opened wide at that. "I'm not so sure that's a wise thing to do. I mean, a sign is one thing, but that is—" Her voice drifted off a little, and she said sheepishly, "I suppose I shouldn't ask for signs either. And certainly not to show someone else's guilt. I'm not sure that's right."

"Well, I wouldn't worry about it. God isn't too likely to answer any prayer of mine."

"Oh, I wouldn't say that."

"I'm just stating the fact." Wade shrugged as he opened the door of his pickup. "We may as well go inside."

The ground was snow-packed and slippery. Wade walked around his pickup so his mother could take his arm as they walked inside.

"The closest stars are out tonight," his mother said when they were almost to the barn's door. She had a thick, wool scarf wrapped around her neck, and she still shivered. "That means there'll be more coming out later, too."

"That'll make it easier to drive the sleigh after dark."

His mother nodded. "Mrs. Hargrove invited me to go home with her and Charley while you take the sleigh around. Charley wondered if you'd need help, so you might want to talk to him about it."

"I think I can handle it alone," Wade said. "It's cold tonight, and I'd hate for Charley to be out in it."

The warmth of the barn made Wade's cheeks tingle when he stepped inside. His mother was rubbing her hands, so she must have felt it, too. A group of young girls in white robes with angel wings on their backs were in the middle of the floor rehearsing what sounded like "Silent Night." The boys, in robes of many different shades of brown, were in a roped-off area trying to keep their dogs calm.

"They still use the bathrobes," his

mother said as she looked around. "I remember Mrs. Hargrove telling me that people donate their old bathrobes and that's how the children all have costumes. They cut the robes down, of course, but Mrs. Hargrove says she always buys a white cotton bathrobe because the angels constantly need more. Maybe the brown bathrobes wear better—those are the ones the men buy."

"Doesn't anyone ever want a bathrobe that's a color? And maybe a silk fabric?" Wade couldn't imagine all of the women in town wearing white cotton robes. He led his mother over to a section of bleachers. There were a handful of parents who were trying to organize the groups of children, but they were so intent on what they were doing, they didn't even look at Wade and his mother.

His mother sat down in the middle of the front row. "The colored robes go for the wise men, especially the shiny ones."

"Ah," Wade nodded as he sat down

next to his mother. He did see, off in the corner, the boys dressed in what looked like silk robes. "They don't seem too happy about being wise men."

His mother smiled. "You know boys. Mrs. Hargrove told me they all want to be shepherds. Or even Joseph, because he gets to lead the donkey in."

"Isn't Mary riding on the donkey?"

"I don't think the boys pay too much attention to that. They like the donkey."

Just then Mrs. Hargrove walked out from behind a curtained area. She had a hairbrush in one hand and a white bathrobe draped over her shoulder. She did see them, though, and hurried over to Wade and his mother.

"I'm so glad you came early," the older woman said as she stood in front of them. "It gets more crowded every year. I think everyone in town will be here tonight. Now that we have a flying angel, we get more people interested."

"Is that the angel who needs the costume?" Wade asked as he nodded toward the robe the older woman had slung over her shoulder.

"Oh, goodness, no. The flying angel wears a special suit that the sheriff's wife made. If you ask me, it looks a little like an astronaut suit. Which is actually good, since the angel doesn't need to worry about being modest if she's in a suit like that. Plus, we have extra padding, because the harness is somewhat uncomfortable without it."

While Mrs. Hargrove was standing there, a woman Wade didn't recognize walked by and handed the older woman a silk robe. "This donation just came in."

"Thank you, Mrs. Redfern," the older woman said with a small frown on her face as she held up the robe. "But I thought we told people no more pink silk robes. The wise men simply won't wear them. One boy threatened to go out there in his father's long johns if all we had for him was one of the pink robes."

The other woman shrugged, looking impatient to leave. "We can't tell people what color of bathrobes they can buy. And that store in Miles City always offers pink robes for Valentine's Day."

"Well, there should be a list of approved bathrobes," Mrs. Hargrove fussed. "We can't have the wise men out there in their long johns. They'd look like beggars instead of men who come bearing precious gifts."

"Oh, no, the gifts," the other woman said as she went rushing off.

"Oh, dear," Mrs. Hargrove muttered as she looked around and then looked down at her hands. "Here," she held out the pink robe to Wade. "Could you hold this?"

Wade didn't really put out his hands, but the robe seemed to be in his lap, anyway.

"This isn't just pink, it's very pink," he said to his mother. "Maybe you could—"

His mother was already grinning. "People will think you're getting in touch with your feminine side."

He snorted. "They'll think I've gone around the bend, and you know it."

When his mother still didn't seem inclined to take the robe, he carefully folded it and set it on the bench beside him. Then he put his Stetson on top of it. The brim of the hat covered most of the fabric.

He and his mother were silent after that. Wade took the time to look around, and he was impressed with the way the barn had been restored without losing its original look. The timbers had been sealed and varnished. The angel pulley was almost hidden in the hayloft. Even the bleachers were built to blend in with the wooden floor, and they weren't high enough to cut off the small windows that lined the wall about eight feet up.

As he recalled, the Elkton ranch had used this barn for roundups at the turn of the century. They'd held their cattle here and in a corral outside until they could sell them. Over time, as shipping was done with trucks instead of horses, the ranch stopped using the barn and the Elkton family finally gave it to the town, calling it a community center.

More people were coming into the building all the time, the men wearing plaid wool coats and the women with knit scarves wrapped around their heads. Everyone's cheeks were pink, and the sound of greetings was drowned out by the shuffling feet of dozens of children.

Wade tried to pick out people that looked somewhat familiar, wanting to be able to greet them by name if they happened to sit near him and his mother. His mother remembered more of the names than he did and would quietly inform him who the people were as they came in the door.

It was almost time for the pageant to begin when Wade realized no one was going to sit beside him and his mother. They had a six-foot circle around them that seemed to be a no-sit zone. People were crowded into the rest of the bleachers, but no one was coming near them.

Wade looked beside him at the pink robe. That thing didn't take up hardly any room, and no one could see it from the doorway, so that wasn't stopping people.

A couple of the ranch hands from one of the local places were even standing by the door, leaning against the wall, because there was no other place to sit down. Wade thought about going over and inviting them to join him and his mother, and then he saw the Mitchells come through the door. Amy was holding one of her grandfather's arms, and her aunt was holding the other.

"They all came," his mother said with pleasure in her voice. She leaned forward as if she was getting ready to go to them. "Maybe they'd like to join us."

"I don't think—" Wade began and let his voice trail off. Maybe the prospect of standing would be enough to bring the

Mitchells over to sit with them. They had the only seating area left.

But then he saw Amy in earnest conversation with her aunt. Aunt Tilly darted a look at him and gave a decided shake to her head.

Wade felt his mother sink back on the bench.

She was silent for a moment, then she spoke. "Mr. Mitchell shouldn't be standing at his age. Maybe if we moved and stood over by the door, they would sit here."

Just then several men sitting near the door stood and waved the Mitchells over.

"Looks like they're taken care of," Wade said.

His mother didn't answer, but they both watched as the three walked over to the seats that had been given to them. Wade looked on as Amy settled her grandfather on the bleachers and then her aunt, as well.

He almost closed his eyes, but then

Amy looked across the room directly at him. He recognized that expression on her face. It was the same one she'd worn when she was ten years old and climbed up on a boulder to jump into the Big Dry Creek for the first time. It had been a particularly wet spring, and the creek had more water in it than usual.

He'd almost had a heart attack that day when he'd realized what she was going to do. He'd thought she'd break her neck for sure. The fact that he had just done it himself hadn't meant anything to him. He'd never wanted Amy to chance being hurt.

And, today the risk was the same.

He stood up, planning to wave her back. But then he saw how many people were watching them. He'd only make it worse if he did something, so he sat back down.

Amy was glad she'd worn her pale blue blouse until she reached up to adjust the collar and noticed the streak of yellow paint on the back of her one finger. The brushes and paint cans she'd taken over to the Stone place had still been on the floorboard of her pickup when her aunt and grandfather had come out of the house tonight to get inside the vehicle.

It had been too late to do anything except move it all to the rear bed of the pickup, so that's what she'd done. The lid on the yellow paint hadn't been on securely, though, and so she'd had to pound it closed with her fist, and then she'd thrown a tarp over all the cans and brushes in hopes the paint wouldn't freeze.

She felt a little self-conscious with the streak of paint on her hand, because it might also be on her nose. She remembered she'd wrapped her scarf around her nose on the drive over to the barn tonight.

No one ever said perfect grooming gave anyone more courage, though, so she took a deep breath and began her walk across the floor of the barn. Someone, probably

Mrs. Hargrove, had taped boundaries on the floor so that the children would know where the edge of the stage area was. She'd used masking tape, and Amy found it easy to follow.

She could feel the eyes watching her, and her shoulder blades started to itch.

Lord, you'd think they've never seen a woman walk before, she complained a little in God's ear, just to keep her nerve up. The whole barn had grown quieter, and she could hear the sound her shoes made on the floor as she kept her eyes looking straight ahead and walked.

Somewhere off in the corner of the barn, a donkey brayed.

Finally, Amy got to her destination.

"Do I have paint on my nose?" she asked Wade as she bent down to move his hat to the side so she could sit beside him.

"What?"

"My nose. Do I have yellow paint on my nose?" she asked and then frowned.

"What are you doing with a pink bath-robe?"

"Don't change the subject," he said, glowering at her.

"What's the subject? Paint or the bath-robe?"

She reluctantly moved the pink silk garment. All she ever bought were white cotton robes because the angels always needed more costumes. She'd almost for-gotten how nice silk felt.

"The subject is you," Wade said.

Which should have sounded romantic, she thought to herself. And it might have if it hadn't been for the thundercloud cov-ering his face.

"I appreciate what you're doing, but you have to live here—these people—" Wade said, his voice low so only she could hear.

"These people will just have to get used to seeing us together." Amy leaned across Wade so she could smile at Gracie. The older woman beamed at her. Then Amy righted herself so she was facing Wade again. "So that's a no on the paint? Any-where on my face?"

"What paint?"

She held up her offending hand. "Paint like this. Do I have any on my nose?"

"Your face is perfect."

Again with the romantic words, Amy thought to herself. Now if he could just work on his delivery, he might actually be convincing.

"What I'm trying to say is that you were right to stay away from me. I'm afraid that—"

"Fear can ruin your life, if you let it," she interrupted him.

And then the sound of a microphone filled the barn.

"Testing. Testing." Charley's voice came through. "Can everyone hear me?"

"You're fine," someone with a deep voice in the audience yelled back. "You're just five minutes late in starting."

"Well, I had to park the sleigh and tie

up the horses," Charley protested. "That takes time and—"

There was a hissing sound in the microphone. Amy thought she might have heard Mrs. Hargrove's voice somewhere in the sounds, but she wasn't sure.

"Oh, well, yeah," Charley continued. "I want to welcome everyone here tonight for the fifteenth annual nativity pageant put on by the children and a few adults from the Dry Creek church. Everyone is welcome to have coffee and cookies after the performance. And, now for the most amazing story ever told. Heeere's Mary and Joseph."

The audience applauded as Charley clicked off the microphone.

Amy watched the donkey come out. Both Joseph and his very pregnant wife were walking and leading the animal. Or, at least, they both had their hands on the reins and looked like they were guiding the donkey in the same general direction.

"Isn't she supposed to be riding the

donkey?" Wade asked in a quiet voice after a moment of watching the slow progress of the three toward the center of the barn.

"The donkey bites," Amy leaned over and told him just as softly. "Sometimes it's hard to find a girl willing to be Mary. This year they made a compromise. Besides, exercise is good for pregnant women."

Wade looked at her and shook his head. "Well, I hope Joseph will step in and rescue her if the donkey looks like it really is going to bite."

"Usually the donkey is bribed enough before she gets onstage that she's well behaved. I think it's a racket. The more the donkey threatens to bite, the more the kids feed her before it all begins."

The angel choir started to sing "O Bethlehem," and the entire barn was quiet.

Amy thought there was something particularly sweet about all those young voices raised in song. They made her feel hopeful.

Someone dimmed the lights, probably to indicate night, once Mary and Joseph found their way to the inn. There was the usual disagreement with Joseph and the innkeeper, and the pageant was underway.

There were no lights over the bleachers, so when the lights were lowered in the middle of the barn, it wasn't easy to see everyone sitting around watching the children perform. Amy took a quick glance over to where she'd left her aunt and grandfather. Her aunt was sitting there, shaking her head at something on the stage. Her grandfather must have stepped out to use the restroom or something, because he was gone. Fortunately, his eyesight was still good so she didn't worry about him not seeing a step and falling.

She was debating whether or not she should go find him and make sure he was safe, when she felt Wade slip his hand into hers. She knew he wouldn't have done it if anyone else was able to see it. She also knew it had no meaning beyond the here and now.

But if she had learned anything from her aunt today, it was to not let the fears of *what might be* interfere with what was happening *now*.

Then, as though it were one of Gracie's signs, the angel Gabriel swung from the hayloft, looked down at the shepherds and shouted, "Fear not, for I bring you tidings of great joy."

Of course, the shepherds tried to look terrified but ended up looking a little comical as they fell to their knees and put their hands to their chests.

There was a scene change as the shepherds got up and switched with the angel choir, so the imaginary curtain was briefly closed.

Wade chuckled softly. "They looked

more afraid of that donkey than of the angel."

"Well, the donkey does bite," Amy reminded him. "As far as I know, Gabriel didn't do anything but appear out of nowhere in the middle of the night."

"That'd be enough to scare me."

"I guess so," Amy said, and she slid a little closer to him.

Being frightened was always eased when you were able to snuggle up next to someone else, she thought, as the shepherds came back onstage and walked to the manger, using their staffs like they were canes.

Chapter Eleven

Wade could have watched the shepherds tend their sheep all night long. He didn't care if he saw the same nondescript brown bathrobe on ten different boys. Amy was by his side, and she liked being there. He was a happy man.

He almost forgot about being a murder suspect, until the wise men walked onstage, each carrying what looked like a bar of solid gold. Seeing so much wealth always made him think of crime.

"I thought there was more than gold," Wade said quietly to Amy. His understanding of the Christmas story was sketchy, but he did remember some strange-sounding gifts that weren't so easily converted into dollars.

"The boys all want to carry the gold," Amy whispered back. "They think frankincense and myrrh are girlie things."

The wise men exited the scene, and there was a lull as the angel choir was being assembled.

"I thought frankincense and myrrh were some kind of scents," Wade said, his voice low even though muffled conversations were happening throughout the barn.

Amy nodded. "Almost perfume. That's got a bad rep with the boys around here."

"Well, they don't have to wear it. They should just carry it to be historically accurate."

"Maybe you'd like to talk to them next year," Amy said quietly and then blushed. "I mean, if you're back here to visit or anything."

"There's no place I'd rather be." He'd

said the words without thinking, but he realized he meant them.

"I might even find a taller tree next year," he added, trying to find some way to say that things would be better if he could make them so by then. "Something more worthy of those ornaments of yours."

"Oh, they're just plain decorations," Amy said.

The angel choir was lined up with their wings on, and they launched into the first verse of "Silent Night."

The barn was not only silent. Wade thought it felt alive with some kind of power.

He let the words of the song seep into his heart as the childish voices rose sweetly to the notes. There truly was something holy about this recreation of the birth of Jesus. It was a wonder that God had come down to earth and let Himself be born in a manger.

I wish I'd known You then, Wade half

prayed, thinking God was a fool to open His arms to men like him. But Wade never was one to turn his back on good fortune. *Help me know You now.* Then he added. *Whatever it takes, Lord. I'm Yours.*

Wade half expected the lights to shine on him when he finished his prayer. Earlier today when he'd thought about it, he'd told himself he should learn more from his reading of the Bible before he made any decisions. But there had been little doubt about his eventual actions, not once he'd started to see the difference faith had made in his mother's life. And now was as good a time as any.

After the angel choir finished, they turned to join the shepherds and wise men in the middle of the barn. All of the children took a bow. Mary, Joseph and the donkey came in from the side of the stage area, and the audience rose to give the cast a standing ovation.

Wade clapped right along with everyone else.

Then lights came on full strength in the barn, and people started milling around.

Wade decided he would wait for a little more privacy before he told his mother and Amy that he'd come to terms with God. He wouldn't have been surprised if they could see some change on his face, but Amy was looking over at where her aunt was standing and muttering something about her grandfather. His mother was standing and looking unsure about where to go next.

"We should go get some refreshments," Wade said.

His mother looked up at him with a question in her eyes.

"We have to keep giving our neighbors another chance until they finally accept us," he said quietly as he set his hat on his head with one hand and picked up the pink robe with the other.

His mother grinned. "Lead the way."

Wade led his mother and Amy toward the refreshment table. Fortunately, Mrs.

Hargrove was at the table, ladling red punch into little plastic throwaway cups. She looked up and greeted them before starting to hand him a cup.

"Don't forget I have your robe," Wade said as he reached out one hand to get the cup of punch that she was offering.

The older woman looked surprised until he lifted up the other hand to show the robe.

"Oh, yes, the pink silk one," the older woman said. "Maybe your mother can bring it over to my place when you make the rounds with the sleigh."

Then Mrs. Hargrove looked back at him. "I wish I had something hot to give you to drink. Some years we have coffee, but this year we're doing good to have the punch ready. We need more volunteers."

"I'd be happy to help," Wade's mother said as she accepted her cup from the older woman, too. "Maybe by next year—" Her voice trailed off.

"I'm sure things will all be sorted out by

then," Mrs. Hargrove said as she handed a cup to Amy.

There was no place to stand while they drank their punch, so the three of them made their way back to where they had been sitting on the bleachers. They had barely gotten settled, though, before Wade knew something was wrong.

There was an agitated stirring among the men in the barn that could only mean something was going on. He wondered briefly if some of the ranch hands had decided to have a brawl outside and then felt ashamed. He had no right to make assumptions about anyone. Not if he planned to live a life of faith like his mother did. She'd learned to see the best in people; he could, too.

He should just sit still and sip his punch, he told himself. Likely all that was happening was that someone had gotten a new pickup and everyone was trying to be the first out the door to kick the tires.

Wade was doing fine with not worrying, until he saw Charley head for the door. The man's face was set in stern lines. Something was bothering him, and it wasn't any pickup.

The thought of Charley in a brawl was what made Wade get up. He didn't want to alarm anyone, so he told his mother and Amy that he wanted to check on the sleigh. Just to be sure he knew where Charley had parked it.

"I'll be back," he said to Amy as he took his empty cup with him.

He tossed the cup in a garbage can just before stepping outside of the barn.

Amy had watched Wade reach the door, and then she turned to Gracie. "Something's wrong."

"That's what I thought," the other woman said.

Amy looked around for her aunt and grandfather and didn't see either one of them.

"Well, it must be happening outside,"

Amy said as she stood up. Wade had left the pink robe behind, and so she picked it up.

"It might be nothing," Gracie said as she got up as well. "But just in case— I don't like to think of Wade out there alone. I mean, I know he's full-grown, but—"

"It's okay," Amy said as she started toward the door. "We'll be there to help."

Amy tried not to worry, but Shawn had called her yesterday and told her to take care of Wade. Then he'd mentioned what had happened in the café and how serious the retired ranchers had been about making sure Wade wasn't doing anything wrong.

The night was dark and, when she first stepped out from the barn, Amy couldn't see very well. She could hear voices, though, and she tried to picture what was happening as the wind blew.

Gracie was right behind her and must be more accustomed to stumbling around in the dark. She touched Amy on the back and guided her over to where the largest cluster of men were lined up as though they were hiding something. Strangely enough, her aunt was standing there with them, wringing her hands.

Amy stifled the urge to caution her aunt about standing in that particular spot. The doctor couldn't have meant for her to do something like that.

Before Amy could say anything to her aunt, she heard Wade start to speak.

"I know you don't trust me," he said, looking at the men. The dark was silent in a way the day never could be.

Even from here, Amy could see that Wade was trying to meet every man's eyes as he went down the line. Most of the men didn't look at him for long.

"I can drive the sleigh safely, though, and deliver the presents for your children," Wade continued as if he was making a promise. "There's nothing to fear."

The line of men didn't waver, though.

They kept standing shoulder to shoulder, looking impenetrable. Amy could see better now, and she knew that what the men were doing was standing in front of the sleigh, as though they were determined to stop Wade from climbing into the driver's seat. The determined looks on their faces said they must think they were saving their children from some horror.

The sound of those very children laughing inside the barn seemed distant. Amy wondered how men could sit through the pageant and come outside into the cold darkness with such hardness in their hearts.

She looked over at Gracie. "I need to go stand with Wade, but I know he wouldn't want you involved in all of this."

"I'm afraid I would only make it worse," the older woman agreed.

Amy nodded. "Please pray, though."

Gracie nodded. "I already am."

Amy hadn't gone more than a few steps

toward Wade when her aunt cried out and came running toward her.

"Don't go to him," Aunt Tilly whispered when she got close. "Something awful—"

Amy didn't stop to listen. Fear had ruled her life long enough. She realized no one had ever stopped her from having a full life. The hesitation and smallness of her life had always been her own doing. She just hadn't reached for anything important for fear she'd lose it, anyway.

When she drew even with Wade, she braced herself.

"Don't send me away," she said quietly. "I know it might hurt to be rejected by our neighbors, but I need to be standing where I am."

Wade looked down at her, his eyes searching hers for a moment. Then he nodded and reached out to take her hand.

"I'm not going to fight you on this," Wade said to the men, his voice deep and patient. "None of us need that."

Then, from somewhere to the side of the barn, Charley came walking into the space between the men and Wade.

"I didn't see anyone out in the trees," he announced to the men.

"Who are you looking for?" Wade asked as he took a step closer to the older man.

All of the men were quiet.

Finally, Charley turned to the wall of men blocking the sleigh. "I think we need to show him. He needs to know what happened."

The men exchanged glances for a minute, and then the line broke as they all stepped to the side so the sleigh was visible.

Amy gasped. "What?"

It was an unnecessary question. It was clear what had happened. Someone had painted the word *murderer* across the side of the sleigh in big, yellow letters. The green elves that danced in the background made the whole sight look eerie.

She felt the shock go through Wade as he read the word, too. Everyone was silent.

"The men weren't trying to stop you from driving the sleigh," Charley finally said. "They just didn't want you to see what someone had done. It's a shameful thing when a community like ours condemns a man without a trial, and the men are sorry for it. They've been cautious, but they mean you and your mother no harm. They asked me to apologize on their behalf for not being friendlier."

Looking awkward, the men stood around the sides of the sleigh for a few minutes.

Finally Wade nodded. "I've got no hard feelings toward anyone."

Amy could feel the tension leave the group of men, and several of them smiled.

Wade must have sensed the change in the group, too, because he said, "I'd be proud to shake any man's hand and begin anew with him."

Now that Wade didn't need anyone to stand with him, Amy turned to leave.

"No," he said as he pulled her closer to him. "Stay."

The men walked over, and soon there was a line of them waiting to shake Wade's hand. Many of them welcomed him home.

The wind was making the night colder, and the stars were beginning to disappear behind clouds. Wade did not care, though. He had never expected to start any new friendships today, and yet he was. The men, from young to old, seemed sincerely sorry they had been slow to show him their friendly side.

He was home.

And he wanted Amy to be with him so she could see for herself that the community was doing their best to accept the Stones back. But she had slipped away, muttering something about her aunt and grandfather. Well, her problems were his now, too, he thought as he set off to find her again.

He only faintly heard someone calling out after him.

Amy had a feeling something was very wrong. She'd glimpsed her aunt at the edge of the darkness, back by the parked vehicles, and there was something frantic about the way she was walking. Aunt Tilly might be doing well tonight, but she was still a sick woman.

The night was darker once Amy walked away from the barn, and she lost sight of her aunt. There was no light spilling out from the windows.

Then she saw movement over by her pickup.

"Aunt Tilly," Amy said as she hurried over.

Her aunt had lifted the tarp off the cans of paint in the bed of her pickup.

"Of course," Amy said as she walked

closer. "Whoever used the paint must have gotten it from here."

Her aunt looked up at her and, even in the dark, Amy could see the tears on the other woman's face.

"It's all my fault," her aunt whispered, agony in every word.

"I'm the one who put the paint back there," Amy said as she stepped closer and enfolded her aunt in her arms.

Amy noticed that her aunt was trembling, though, and something was still not right. So she patted her aunt on the shoulder. "You are talking about the paint, aren't you?"

Then Amy looked over and saw the silhouette of her grandfather in the window of the pickup. He was sitting there, not moving.

Amy felt, more than saw, her aunt shake her head.

"It's not the paint," the woman finally said. "It's—" Her aunt stopped.

Then Amy saw Wade walking toward

them. And several men following
im over.

"What is it then?" Amy focused on her
aunt again.

It was silent for a moment and then her
aunt gave a sob and cried out. "He's the
one."

At first, Amy thought her aunt was ac-
cusing Wade of something again, but she
followed the other woman's gaze, and she
wasn't looking at him.

"Grandfather?" Amy asked. "Are
you saying he painted that word on the
sleigh?"

Her aunt nodded. "He's got paint all
over his hands."

"But why—" Amy began and then gave
up. Her family would never accept Wade,
and she'd just have to live with it.

Her aunt hadn't stopped though. She
kept crying, but her words came out clear.
"He's the one who killed Buck Stone."

Everything went silent. Amy was
vaguely aware of Wade and several other

men standing around, but she felt a rushing in her ears. She felt like nothing made sense. "But why would grandfather kill Mr. Stone?"

"It was because of me," her aunt said, deep and low. "He found out that Buck and I were, well, having an affair. Grandpa thought Buck was the only one at fault. I tried telling him it wasn't all Buck."

Her aunt took a deep breath and looked at Amy. "I swear I didn't think Grandpa had killed him. Not when Gracie confessed. I thought Grandpa's nightmares were making him imagine things. His mind was already mixed up. So when he told me he'd done it, I told him he hadn't. I thought he just had a bad dream because of what Gracie had done."

Amy felt Wade step closer and put his arm around her.

She turned to look at him. "You heard everything?"

He nodded.

"What do we do?" Amy whispered.

"First, we get your aunt someplace warm," Wade said, the kindness in his voice almost making her weep. "Then we put your grandfather to bed for the night. We'll let Sheriff Wall know what your aunt said and let him take it from there."

Amy nodded.

Then Wade turned to speak to someone else, and Amy noticed that most of the men from the sleigh were standing there in the darkness, waiting for him to say something.

"We don't need to be rushing to any conclusions here," Wade said to the men. "But I do think we've had enough excitement for the night." He looked over at Charley then. "I'm afraid I won't be able to drive the sleigh after all. Maybe someone else can volunteer."

"Nobody can drive it tonight, anyway," Charley said. "Not with that word painted on it the way it is."

"Why doesn't Wade just drive it out in

the morning?" one of the other men said. "We'll tell the kids that the sleigh needs some repairs and they can expect their presents in daylight this year."

"I could do that," Wade said and the men murmured their agreement.

Then he looked down at Amy. "Would you come with me for an early morning ride?"

She nodded her head.

Wade got to her house before the sun had risen, but Amy was dressed and waiting for him. Her aunt and grandfather were both tucked securely into their beds and sleeping well. So many questions had been answered last night. She now knew why her aunt had changed. She felt guilty for the affair, and suspected it had lead to murder, even though she thought it was Gracie who had killed Buck. The secret had eaten away at her, and she couldn't bear to think about the Stone family.

Amy didn't wait for Wade to come to

the door. She met him halfway, and they went back to the pickup.

They drove to Charley's to pick up the sleigh, and the older man was waiting for them in his shop with a thermos of hot cocoa for their ride.

"We had lots of volunteers last night who came to repaint the sleigh," Charley said.

Every trace of the yellow paint was gone. And then Amy saw the elves. "They're wearing cowboy hats!"

She started to laugh.

Wade hooked up the horses to the sleigh and they were on their way just as the sun was starting to rise. Charley had given them an old quilt to put on their laps so they'd keep warm. A steady flurry of snow fell.

"This is a Christmas fit for a new beginning," Wade said as he drove on one of the side roads. Ahead of them everything was covered in white.

Amy nodded. "You and your mom will have it much easier from now on."

Wade was silent for a bit then he pulled the horses to a stop. He turned and looked at her. "I meant a new beginning for you and me."

"If you can forgive me for not trusting you during all of this," Amy said, the words tumbling out of her. "I should have—"

"There's nothing to forgive," Wade said simply as he looked down at her.

"But all those years," Amy said. "You had forgotten me and then—"

Wade smiled at that. "I guess I should have said there's no need for you to ask my forgiveness. I should be asking yours though. It wasn't that I didn't think about you during all of that time—"

Amy looked at him skeptically. By now, the sun was rising farther in the sky.

"I can prove it," he said with a grin as he opened his coat and reached into the pocket of his shirt. He pulled out a packet of spearmint gum.

She was astonished. "They don't even make that color of wrapper anymore."

"I know," he said. "I don't chew it. I just keep it to remind me of you."

Amy felt the smile start deep inside and move to her face. "You're saying an old packet of gum makes you think of me? Some men would go for roses. Or diamonds. Or even the stars in the sky—"

Wade started to laugh and his eyes turned golden.

"From now on I don't plan to need that gum," he said as he moved his head closer to hers. "Not when I have you."

He moved his head closer to her. "I love you, Amy Mitchell."

His breath warmed the cold air around them as she looked up at him. The horses stood still and even the snow stopped. Everything was quiet around the sleigh.

"You do?" Amy whispered. She'd waited for this moment for almost ten years. But now that it was happening, she felt her insides clench together like she was going to faint.

Wade nodded. "And I plan to tell you that every day for the rest of our lives." He hesitated. "That is, if you'll have me."

He looked away then as though he was unsure of his answer. The sun shone full on his face and showed up every worry line and whisker.

"I know I don't have much to offer," he continued and suddenly his words were coming out fast. "But I'm determined to make something of the ranch and I have some savings from the rodeo—quite a bit of savings actually. Enough to build us a good house and—"

Then, he stopped and lifted his eyes. "You're not saying anything. I don't mean to rush you." He looked away again. "I know it's sudden. We were kids when we… Well, I understand if you don't feel the same way anymore. All I ask is a chance to prove myself. You don't have to make any decisions about us until you're ready."

Amy saw him reach for the reins. She refused to let this moment pass.

"Wait," she gasped, and then forced herself to take a deep breath.

Wade's hands stopped moving and he turned back to look at her. "You okay?"

She took another breath just to steady herself.

"I'm more than okay."

"Good," Wade said, although he still looked hesitant. "Because you really don't have to worry about rushing into anything."

Amy put her finger up to his lips to stop him.

Then she cleared her throat. "If you make me wait another ten years, Wade Stone, I'm going to refuse to talk to you ever again. I love you, too."

His rich laugh rang out and Amy felt the tension leave her.

"I expect we can rush a little," he finally said as he pulled her closer to him and leaned down. "Especially since it's Christmas."

His lips met hers and Amy wondered if it was the elves she heard sighing in delight. Then she decided it had been her after all.

* * * * *

Dear Reader,

When I began the story of the Stone family, I knew I wanted to touch on the problems people have when they try to go home. Those difficulties can seem even more pronounced at Christmas than at other times of the year.

I have received emails from enough readers to know that the holidays can be difficult for many of us. That's why I always urge the readers of my Christmas books to find a church where they can attend services. We are all part of the family of God, and that's never more real than when we celebrate the birth of Our Lord together.

So have a blessed Christmas this year. Reflect on what He means to all of us.

And, if you have a minute, I would love to hear from you. Just go to my website, www.janettronstad.com, and email me from there.

Sincerely,

Janet Tronstad

Questions for Discussion

1. Wade Stone came back to Dry Creek because he was worried about his mother, Gracie. What would you think if someone recently released from prison settled in your neighborhood? Would you welcome them?

2. How would Jesus react to living next to an ex-con? Can you think of any verses in the Bible that show how Jesus reacted to lawbreakers?

3. Wade left Dry Creek after his mother's trial without saying goodbye to his friends because he was ashamed of his family. If you could have counseled with him, what would you have told him?

4. Gracie became a Christian while in prison. Do you know of someone who

has become a Christian in prison? How about becoming a Christian in other difficult situations?

5. Gracie relied on signs to know God's will. Do you agree that God speaks to us in that way? Why or why not?

6. Gracie told Wade that the truth would set him free. How is that shown in the book?

7. Amy Mitchell spent her years taking care of her aunt and her grandfather. At the beginning of the book, she felt like life was passing her by. Have you ever been called upon to perform a duty that made you feel like your life was on hold?

8. Charley and Mrs. Hargrove welcomed the Stones back home to Dry Creek. Why do you think the whole town didn't welcome them?

9. Amy struggled to believe in Wade's innocence. Have you ever known someone who was accused of a major crime? Tell us about it.

10. Wade had always wanted to drive the Christmas sleigh in Dry Creek because it was a fond memory from childhood. Do you have a dream of something you would like to do on Christmas?

11. The gifts were an important part of the Christmas sleigh. I believe that giving gifts on Christmas is a way of opening ourselves up to the friendship and love of others. How do you feel when you give a gift to someone? When you receive when?

12. Which character in the book did you most identify with when reading it? Why?